ONLY FOR HIM

THE ONLY SERIES: VOLUME ONE

CRISTIN HARBER

New York Times and *USA Today* Best Selling
Author

MILL CREEK PRESS

ISBN-10: 1-942236-12-3
ISBN-13: 978-1-942236-12-2

www.CristinHarber.com

CHAPTER ONE

Sophomore Year,
Summerland County High School…

Grayson

This entire shitty-ass trailer reeks. The stink of cheap liquor and an even cheaper woman hangs in the air as I walk in the door. There's a system I keep for knowing how deep Pops is, and it goes by smell. If he's been smokin' pot, I'm on my own before football practice. No big deal. If the stench of cheap beer fills our place, Pops'll give me hell, but not enough that I can't duck out and escape. I'll be a little banged up, but nothing I can't ignore when Coach Snyder makes me run laps for being late. But if our trailer smells like liquor, I'm screwed.

That's the last thing I need. I forgot my damn football pads this morning and needed to slink in, grab them, and go. But judging by what stinks, that may've been a bad decision.

"Oh!" A woman's slurred surprise drifts down the short hall.

Well... damn.

I turn toward the source of the slurred yip and cheap vanilla aroma. She walks into the room, and I feel her gaze as I assess her level of sobriety. On a scale from buzzed to smashed, she's hovering around a solid tipsy. Smeared red lipstick and years' worth of smoking are written on her too-tan face. That's Pops's type—dive bar skank.

The lady's hair screams "just been fucked," and she hops from one foot to the other, tugging on a stripper-girl shoe. One foot makes it into the see-through plastic, but she drops to the ragged carpet in a mess of drunken giggles.

Great.

"Hey, you," she slurs, her eyes bobbing all over me.

Disgusting. I don't know her name, but I could guess. Bambi. Candi. Mandi. Sandi. I think they make up their names. Statistically, there aren't enough parents in Summerland County naming their kids with names ending in i to allow his screws to all rhyme.

"Didn't know you had a boy, Randall," she coos, more to me than to Pops. "Quite the boy..."

Not only have I been caught at home, but the lady is eyeball fuckin' the shit out of me. Pops's instability makes him jealous, which fuels his anger. Like I'd touch one of his whores.

But now that Pops is done with his woman, he's going to take it out on me for whatever he dreams up—that I'm flirting with his fucks or that I... exist. *Such an asshole.* I exist. I'm his son. His problem. It blows my mind how often he brings his trash back here when he doesn't want them to know I'm alive. In what world does that make sense?

Shirtless and with glassy eyes, Pops sways from the back room, acting drunk and well-fucked. I hate that look; I always thought that getting laid should chill him out, but it never does. Just makes him angrier. Not that it is hard to do. He can go from passed-out to ready-to-kill in a liquor-stinking breath.

Pops sneers at me, and even though I should expect it, my stomach sinks. He hates me, and as sick as it is, I can't blame him. I ruined our lives.

"Grayson, boy, told you not to come home."

"Randall." The lady, still sitting on her butt, giggles from the floor. "You're too young for a boy that big." She eyes me like she needs another go in Pops's waterbed. Alcohol-fueled lust fires behind her makeup-caked eyelashes.

My skin crawls. Her tongue darts out, licking like she wants to taste me, and a foul shiver runs through me.

Pops swings his glare between me and his piece of ass, and his scowl tightens. "You shoulda stayed doing your football, ROTC, whatever the fuck you do. Not come here."

If I didn't need my shit for football, I wouldn't have come home. I should've skipped practice. I'm never going to make it back in time. With the anger pulsing in our trailer, there's no doubt Pops wants a fight that I won't give him. I can't—I've earned every punch he lands.

Dread rushes into my blood. The thing about a whiskey punch is that it hurts a fuckava lot more than if he's been slamming beers. Even better is when he's stoned. Even if his limp-dick fist balls, there's a good chance he'll pass out before he makes contact.

I swallow the lump in the back of my throat, bracing for what will come. It will suck, especially since he doesn't seem *that* drunk. The more sober he is, the longer he lasts. A shitty fact of life. The guy's up for father of the year.

"I forgot my pads." I try to sidestep him in the narrow living-slash-kitchen area.

He takes two swaying steps. "Boy." Spittle hits the back of my neck, then his fist cracks sloppily on my head.

Son of a bitch. I hadn't braced for that. If a hit's coming, I zone out, not feeling a thing. But him swinging in front of that lady? I shrug it off, ignoring the sting. "Just getting my shit, and I'm out, Pops."

"You ain't goin' nowhere now, boy."

I move toward my room. Practice is in twenty minutes. My teeth grind together. If I can just—

Pops grabs my shoulder, steadying himself, and then leans in. "I said—"

"Think I should be going." The woman gives a smoker's cough.

Even though bench-pressing his weight would be easy, I let Pops whirl me to the counter. It takes everything I have to detach. The counter edge digs into my back, and I know the beating is coming. The confirmation is in his eyes, and one long onceover tells me he's not nearly drunk enough to make this session quick.

I've had fifteen years walking this earth, and I should've known better than trying to sneak in to grab my gear. I'm never going to make practice tonight. Coach Snyder might wonder, but he never asks.

"You knew I had company, you little shit." His voice is cigarette stained. More spittle hits my skin. "Honey," Pops calls to the lady without taking his eyes off me. "I'll call you. Get your ass goin' home now."

"'Kay, honey." She fumbles toward the door, swinging a purse off the couch.

The honey-talk makes me sick. Maybe she doesn't think he'll fight, and I'll just take it. I have a couple inches on him, plus muscle where he has none. I play sports. He smokes anything he can find. I survive on protein bars. Pops trades our food stamps for dime bags and fifths of whatever burns the hardest. Instinct should have my adrenaline going, readying to fight or flight. But it doesn't.

"What's wrong with you?" Pops snaps.

Everything.

But I shake my head slowly and wait, daring him to strike. I'm not afraid of pain. Maybe I even embrace it.

My heart pounds for all the wrong reasons. This is what I deserve but can't wait to escape. As the trailer door slaps shut, he drives home a gut shot.

The hit explodes. I torture myself by staying under his roof, knowing he's the most pathetic, ruined man I've ever met. But I made him that way, and as fucked up as it sounds, it's the only way I think he'll survive. I owe him that much. Long ago, Pops was normal... I was normal... Mom was alive.

Another blow lands, and my breath is gone. I brace for his wheezy left hook. It connects, but I've already started to numb out, thinking the only thoughts that save me from my nightmare.

The sweaty stench of liquor registers as he lands a slap. "Fuck you, boy."

Another slap to my temple, and he grabs my ear, ripping it down. A burn of pain explodes, and I silence my reaction, dropping to my knees. His drunken attack hits more than it misses. The scalp shots hurt, blistering fresh pain into a familiar headache. Blood touches my tongue. Bruises are a part of life. No one looks too hard. This is what I've accepted.

Harder punches rain down, but I'm gone. Numb. I hear the swings more than I feel the impact. I wonder if this is how soldiers detach when they're prisoners of war. I close my eyes and think about the only thing that makes life worth the trials: Emma Kingsley, her sweet smile, and the laugh that make me believe in a future.

Warmth bleeds through me, and I'm aware of her innocence. Sophomore year isn't for finding answers in a girl's face. It's for working my way off first-string JV and figuring out how to pass chemistry.

Another hit strikes my temple. Pops nails that perfect spot, and my balance is off. Pain I will not admit to explodes behind my eyes. Another strike lands. Then a push. I'm down on my back. Violent agony ricochets as Pops's bare foot strikes my ribs. That bastard.

Emma.

I fight to think of her. The only girl I want. The only one I could ever tell about this. But I won't.

I open my eyes. It's the wrong time to say I'm sorry. Our gazes clash, then one sloppy kick flies to my head. A hair of a second before his foot hits, I know I'm going to be out.

CHAPTER TWO

JUNIOR YEAR...

EMMA

Irish twins. The thing about sharing classes with my older brother is that we confuse people. Ryan is eleven months older than me. Most assume we are fraternal twins, since we don't look *at all* the same. His hair is dark blond. Mine's more gold. His eyes are hazel; mine are brown. He's a little preppy, a little trendy, which is a good combination on him. But I'm all over the place: maxi dress one day, a jeans-and-shirt combo that's more tomboy than casual the next.

Tonight, it's torn-at-the-knees jeans and a screen-print tee with a pixelated, monochrome design I'd made in photography class. All around me, music thumps. Some of the guys from our class are getting trashed. Some of the girls are, too. But mostly, it's just a typical party.

Courtney and Melanie are in the corner, evil-eyeing me, but I catch them, and they glance away. There's a good chance they're in deep discussion about revoking my BFF card. Fine by me. I just want to leave, and that's why I'm getting their dirty looks. I'm distracted by one Grayson Ford, hottest guy in the room, and my platonic best guy friend. Yay…

He's got a cheerleader following him around, and he isn't ignoring her. Yay, again.

"Hey." Hands clap to my shoulders and spin me around. Courtney's glaring at me. "Would you just go over there already?"

I can't even play dumb. "Nah. What's the point?"

Melanie sidles up. "Yeah, what's the point? Except you two are like star-crossed lovers or something—crazy in love and doing nothing about it."

Crazy love. I've grown up with the perfect example of that. And *that* is not *anything* that I have with Gray. Well, at least it's not mutual because, whether I admit to it or not, I love him and have since I can remember.

Courtney throws her head back, laughing. "First comes love—" Melanie joins in with their rhyme, and in sync, they finish up, "Then comes babies in a baby carriage."

They break into squeals about our future imaginary children. God. But I'm not even going to have this discussion. Pointing to my ear, I mouth, "What? Never..."

My parents *are* crazy in love and, apparently back in the day, humped like rabbits. Totally disgusting, except for kind of cute, which is why there were three of us kids in very short order. Cherry is about a year older than Ryan, and she's the wild child.

Our folks stopped after me, probably because three kids three and under would be enough to send anyone to an asylum. Mom's sanity was likely saved from the loony bin by tying her tubes—which incidentally was the only time our parents would ever, even in passing, touch on the birds and the bees talk. Win-win for all. I like being the baby of the family, our parents are sane, and no one had to sit around for an awkward conversation.

But why I'm thinking about families and babies while staring at Grayson out of the corner of my eye is... pathetic. He's Ryan's best bro and a semi-permanent fixture around our house. Grayson is just Grayson, and even if I've imagined him looking at me the way I do him, it's just not a possibility.

So I'm glad he and Ryan are tight. I'm even happier that I can at least call him my close friend, too. I focus on our long standing friendship. It's been the only way I can justify the homicidal tendencies that provoke my inner ninja warrior chick every single time I see some bippy-boppy, cliquey bitch succeed in capturing his attention.

"Seriously, Emma. You need to chill out or head home." Courtney hip-bumps me.

"Can't." I turn to her, shaking my head. I've masochistically offered to make sure both Ryan and Grayson have a sober ride at the end of the night. And by sober ride, I mean me.

"Right. Well, don't look now, but here comes a certain somebody." Melanie giggles into her red plastic cup. "See ya."

Courtney squeaks. "Eek, see ya!"

They both take off in the absolute most obvious way possible. *Shit, shoot, shit.* Deciding that my thoughts are too transparent, I head for the front door. Some fresh air will fix me up since I'm pretty much the only sober person here.

"Emma?" Grayson calls from behind me.

I pretend like I don't hear and push through the crowd for the door. I'm almost outside when I hear Ryan calling after me, too. He's laughing, and once I'm on the front yard, I turn around to see my brother heading out the door with his arm thrown around a girl I pretty much hate. "Let's go to Whities before we drop them home."

Them? Oh, no. I didn't sign up to chauffeur around Ryan and that girl making out all over the back seat while trying to ignore Grayson, who's looking ten kinds of amazing. And... no way am I heading for a burger run. Just not gonna happen.

The door to the house opens again, and out walks Grayson. My mind freezes then spirals to an immediate love-struck-heartbroken twist when I see Gray with *another her* whom I dislike. Immensely.

She's clinging to his broad chest and giggling as they make their way down the front porch. I hate this, how I feel, how I react. There's always that distant, maybe-one-day kind of hope that this weird vibe is actually not a made-up daydream. But if that's the case, why would he torture me?

"Ems." He shoves away from his clinger. "We leaving?"

At least that shove gives me some very small level of satisfaction, even though she just moves back in again.

"Hey." I jingle my keys then turn to Ryan. "Yes. But we're not going to Whities."

Ryan groans, and I roll my eyes.

Gray sidesteps the girl on his hip. "Why'd you run off a sec ago?"

"I was in sober-girl hell." *No way will I admit to him why.* Everywhere I went tonight, there was a chick trying for his attention.

"So why'd you run for the door just now?" His voice is teasing. He nudges my shoulder with his arm.

I swear, between those arms and that chest, I don't know what to do with myself. I shrug instead, imagining him holding his arm around me, pressing our bodies together. "I was bored. Didn't want to drink, and I have dance in the morning."

My list makes sense, but none of it's true. I can't drink around Grayson for fear that I'll do something stupid. And I like being their sober option because I'm pretty much their *only* option, and that guarantees me more time with him. I'm a Grayson Ford addict. No one will blame me though, and I'm pretty sure there's an *I Dream of Gray* support group at school.

My eyes slide over him. He's perfect. Sweet. Funny. Smart. Tough. A combination of male awesomeness, all in the right blend.

The girl who had been latched to Ryan's chest pulls back from him. "Seriously, Emma, you should try out for the team."

Now the girl under Gray's arm scowls. "Try-outs have been over for forever."

Add her snippy shut down of something I don't even want to do to the list of reasons I hate her.

Ryan's girl smiles at me, and I think that she's actually trying to suck up to me to win him over. "For Emma's talent, I think we'd make an exception." Spoken like a true captain of the cheerleading squad.

Whatever. Art bleeds in my veins. I know I could do well on the cheerleading team, but that's not why I dance. The rhythm, the feelings, with the right music and a focus, I don't dance. I emote. All that poetry in motion stuff comes naturally to me.

"She's not a dancer," Grayson adds. "She's a photographer."

Dancing's fun, but photography is who I am. He knows it. Heat hidden by the evening's dim light hits my cheeks. "That I am. But really, I'm your ride, so in the car. Let's go."

Grayson's girl wraps her arms on him, readying to work some take-me-home magic. But he sidesteps her move, and relief floods me.

"Hey." Gray points down the street. "Becca's in your neighborhood. She'll drop you."

When her mouth hinges open to protest, he leans in to add a more private part to their conversation. Whatever he said works, and after a bit of giggle-fussying, she waves goodbye and almost skips down the sidewalk.

Seriously. I. Hate. Her. Or maybe it's me that I'm hating. Why can't I just tell him? Sighing, I know the answer I've replayed a million times.

He's my friend.

My *best* friend.

It will ruin everything. He's Grayson Ford, the dream boyfriend, the ideal catch. And I'm me: cute but not gorgeous, friendly but not super popular. If Ryan wasn't my brother, I wonder if as many people would even notice I exist. A long time ago, I learned that some *friends* only wanted to hang with me for access to Ryan and Gray. Nice.

Back to chauffeur duty. Ryan's attached at the face to his cheerleader and heading toward the back seat.

Grayson throws his arm around my shoulder and leans in. His lips graze my temple, evidence that he's had his share of keg beer and laughs. "Take me home, Emma."

Ha. If he had *any* clue.

CHAPTER THREE

Emma

A million middle-of-the-night conversations passed through our adjoining air vent as I lay on my bed and my sister Cherry did the same in her room. She used to tell me secrets through the slats while we knocked our heels against the wall and chatted in the dark.

I'm sure our deep, giggles were broadcast to the entire house. They probably gave our folks heart failure because, even when Cherry was a kid, she was a handful. Mom would come up and tell us to go to bed. Dad would come up and tell us to stop scuffing the walls—but then he'd tuck us in. Twenty seconds later, we'd be on our backs again, feet in the air, knocking and scuffing and telling secrets.

When Cherry left for college, everything changed. I lost my sounding board. She might be three years older, but she was my confidant. I saw the world vicariously through her eyes. She never had a negative outlook on life, never thought she wasn't the center of attention, but she always held my hand, doling out amazing, albeit unconventional advice. I really miss her.

Lying on my back with Grayson on my mind, I look at the vent and knock my heels against the wall, trying to imagine what Cherry would say about the debacle at lunch today—

Knock, knock.

I turn my head, and there's my problem. In the span of a second, my languid musings about my festering crush are replaced by the slow mind-meld that is Grayson Ford.

"Hey, Gray." I swear, each day he grows bigger, and his eyes become more vibrant. All he does is work out. Baseball season is about over, yet he's training like he's eyeing the Olympics. I don't get it, but I'm able to appreciate the benefits of his grueling regimen.

"Hey, you. We've gotta talk."

My stomach drops as I swallow the burst of lust that I've become accustomed to when he shows up. I sit up from probably the most unattractive position: legs up, head down, kicked back on my bed. Or maybe it's the most provocative, if I were the provocative type. *I wish I were.*

His eyes track my legs to my face. I really shouldn't lie upside down if there's even the slightest chance he'll show up. A fire heats up my neck and into my cheeks. I don't have a clue about the type of flirting that would be in Gray's league. When it comes to him, I'm an expert on unrequited desire. Perks of being just a friend...

"You ran out of school today like your ass was on fire." He bounds a couple huge steps and flops down next to me. The entire bed shifts, and the addictive scent of his soap invades my space.

I turn to my side and take in his profile. Shower-wet hair, cheeks that are starting to chisel as he grows into a physique that doesn't look remind me of any other guy's in our school. He's more of a man every day, and I feel more like an awkward nerd girl.

"Tell me you're not pissed about earlier." He turns to his side to face me, and I bite my lip. He takes up most of my twin bed. Mom and Dad would freak if it were anyone but Grayson. Their "no boys in my room" rule was carved into stone during my freshman year when Ryan's friends started hanging around—sniffing around, as Dad says. But I say that's a big, fat laugh. Their room-rule doesn't apply to Gray, though.

He reaches over our heads and grabs my iPod, shoving an ear bud in his ear and one in mine. A few scrolls later, music blasts. It's kinda emo, a little deep, nothing that I expect he'd choose. The vocals croon about heartache, about how the future is a blur. The beat drops low, and the bass rolls through my body. Even though Gray's so close, or maybe because of it, I feel my blood thumping.

"Now that..." Slowly, he nabs the lone ear bud from me. Our eyes lock. "I'd pay to see you dance to."

"Grayson," I whisper as a fever hits my neck, bleeding through me. When he looks like this— acts like it too—I don't know what's for real and what's in my head.

"Been talking to your wall?"

I stifle a cringe. He knows me so well it hurts. "Something like that."

"About me?" He smiles, but it's not a joke. Everything feels different. His voice sounds different. His touches have been longer, his stares deeper, and right now, he's not pulling back from his question. "Nothing to say, Ems?"

Without an answer to give him, I roll back to stare at the ceiling.

He groans. "You're mad at me, right?"

Shoot. We're going to have to talk about today. But I'm clueless. It's like having what I want served on a platter, but it's not real.

He nudges my shoulder. "Say something."

If I stay quiet another second, he's going to think I'm nuts. Protecting my heart is my top priority, but I can't let go of the hope. "Kelly Reynolds will probably hate me for the rest of my life."

It's the best thing I've got, talking about something besides him and me but staying on topic. Not bad. But Grayson's deep laugh surrounds me.

I turn to face him again, and his brilliant smile makes his perfect face radiate. "Kelly Reynolds is a slut."

True, but that isn't my issue with her. "She thinks I asked you to Sadie Hawkins."

"You were going to." Confident and handsome. The total package.

"Oh, my God." I can't breathe. What the hell's going on between us? *Downplay, downplay, downplay.* I can't handle him right now. Smiling like he's dropping jokes, I nudge him back. "No way. You were bottom of my list, seriously, deep on the backup pile if I couldn't nab a date."

A brooding scowl darkens his face. "Like you couldn't swing any date you wanted."

"Not quite..."

He elbows me but lingers longer than he should. The heavy beat of my pulse thumps in my neck. I feel it in my wrists, and my mouth waters. What is it with us?

"Shit, Ems. I don't know what to do here."

I jerk back. Wait. What? My stomach's in my throat, my skin has shiver bumps, I can't inch away, and he's not moving.

"Gray?" But I forget everything else I want to say because I want to hear him say those words again. Then I'll believe that whatever this is I feel is not just in my head.

He pushes a few strands of hair off my cheek, and it's surreal. My breaths are shallow. My mind races. Confliction and confusion battle for fore-front in my mind. He's the only boy I'll ever trust enough to blush in front of, if that makes sense, which it doesn't. I blame stupid love.

"Tell me a story, Emma." He inches closer. "Tell me something that takes us far away from here."

That's his thing. He hates *here*, which I don't entirely get. But he loves that I'm a dreamer, that I can transport us far away when we close our eyes. It's something we've done since we were kids, and even when I can't breathe lying next to

him, the familiarity is as intoxicating as it is sooth-
ing.

Okay. I can do this. "Eyes closed, Gray."

"Closed."

I breathe in deeply and think of something that
moves us away from now. I can't think of anything
because I've never loved a moment as much as
this one.

"Are your eyes still closed, Emma?"

They are. I nod. "Yup."

There's a shift of his weight as he moves on
the bed, coming closer. "Keep them closed."

My lungs ache. My heart's exploding, and my
senses are hyper-alive. My lips part, wanting to
tell him a story, wanting to kiss him more than I
want to breathe. My eyelashes flutter.

"*Closed*, Ems." His low voice rakes over me.

I'm dying. In heaven. Right now.

His side touches my side. The heat from his
body covers mine. His soft breaths torture my
cheek... my chin... then hover over my lips.

Unable to control myself, I feel my hips shift.
My chin tilts up. Anticipation squeezes deep into
my soul. He's watching me. My eyes are still shut,
but I can feel his gaze as his finger touches my
hair, sliding down the strands to the slope of my
collarbone.

I'm ready—swooning, melting, *panting*—for a kiss.

"God, you are beautiful, Ems," he whispers.

My eyes open, and my mind spins. The vibrant green of his are inches away.

"What are we doing?"

"I'm memorizing what takes me away. What saves me."

"You've—" My whispering voice cracks, but I don't care how I sound. I'm toeing the cusp of all I ever wanted.

"We're done ignoring us." His hand cups my face, fingers stroking my cheeks down to my chin. When my lips part, his eyes drop to my mouth, focusing on my lips.

I've been kissed. Dates. Dares. However they've happened, I've had a few solid moments of PG-rated hookups. *Nothing* I have *ever* experienced has *anything* on this moment, and Gray's lips haven't even touched mine.

His heavy weight lies atop of me, but one arm props him up, so I'm not crushed. I can't think. Just feel. A kiss has never been more meant to be. Then his lips touch mine. I breathe him in.

He groans into my mouth, and I let his tongue sweep mine. Hungry for more of him, I wrap my arms around his shoulders, scarcely believing this is happening. Knowing how big and broad Gray is, that's one thing. Wrapping myself around him, feeling him hold me, kiss me—it's insane.

His hands thread into my hair, and it's like we've unleashed a fire. His hips flex to mine. His erection pushes into my stomach. Without thought, I'm biting his lip, scratching my fingers into his back—

A noise startles us. We're frozen, panting, connected and staring into each other's eyes.

"Garage," I mumble against his lips.

He hugs me close; then we separate, rolling to opposite ends. All I can do is stare at Grayson and smile like a loon.

He chuckles and tilts his head, a crooked half smile on his face. "What—"

The bedroom door opens. Dad and Ryan were out running some kind of man-errands that I wasn't invited to and didn't want to go on. Thank God.

"Hi, sweetie pie." My dad pops his head in. "Oh, hey, Grayson." Then Dad laughs like what just happened has no chance of ever happening between Gray and me. "No boys in your room with the door closed."

"Hey, Mr. Kingsley."

"Right. Gotcha. Sorry." The way those three words fumble out of my stuttering mouth should've been a neon blinking sign that screamed obvious. But apparently, Dad's stuck in oblivious mode.

"I meant to tell you, son, great job last Friday." Then Dad smiles at me. "Guess this guy will always be an exception in this house."

He turns to leave, *shuts the door*, and there Grayson and I are, still silent and staring. I slap my hands over my mouth, certain insane, nervous giggles are going to explode at any second. Gray's the epitome of cool collectedness. Must be nice.

Pound, pound. Ryan thumps on my door as he walks past. "Gray in there?"

Grayson's eyes trail toward the door, then he stands. "So..."

"So..." Please don't ruin anything. Please don't say anything like *whoopsie* or *oh, shit, why did that happen*?

He leans against my wall, and his green eyes are on fire. A smile that melts me catches on his lips. "Get ready to get your Sadie Hawkins on."

My mind is already doodling *Mrs. Grayson Ford* in imaginary notebooks. He has no clue where my head is. But given that I didn't see what just happened coming *at all*, maybe I have no clue where his head is either.

He lifts his chin to say goodbye. Then he's gone. Down the hall, Grayson and Ryan bro out. I listen to their muffled voices while I press my fingers against my mouth. My lips feel swollen. My entire body feels… explosive.

Finally, I drop back to my bed and kick my feet up. Cherry needs to weigh in on this situation. I grab my phone and see a text message from Grayson.

Grayson: *No more stories. That's all I've ever needed.*

CHAPTER FOUR

EMMA

I'm so glad this week is over. After kissing Gray and walking around like a grinning lovesick puppy for about twenty-four hours, I immediately realized I was going to screw this up. For the rest of that day, I hid in my room, blowing up Cherry's phone with emergency SOS texts. When she called me, her advice was perfect. Then she dropped the same message, but a thousand times more concise, into a text.

Cherry: *Whatever you do, don't let him go. He's perfect.*

Yeah, no kidding. But how wasn't I going to screw up? I have no idea what to do about kissing Gray, other than finding a kickass dress for Sadie Hawkins. Then I scroll back to her next text.

Cherry: *What are you gonna tell Ryan?!*

The thing is Ryan would handle it well. We're all friends, and Gray's not a dick. Still, telling Ryan, that's unnerving. But there's nothing to tell Ryan if I can't pull my act together and stop avoiding Gray.

I've been a complete baby about it. In my defense, it was the world's most perfect kiss. I still get the feels thinking about it. As far as I can tell, there's a significant chance that it can't get any better than it was in my bed.

Well, in my imagination, it can. But real life?

Sadie Hawkins is tomorrow night, and I have no choice but to see him since I'm his date and all. Shit. The slow pound of my heart begins its predictable cadence, thinking of the dress that took three days of shopping to find. The blue fabric and curving fit have one purpose: explain to Grayson what I want when I can't manage to talk.

Scrolling back to Cherry's text—shit—I catch the time, and I'm late. I grab my camera bag and bolt downstairs. If there's any way I'm going to hit the sunset that curves over Three Sisters Mountain, I needed to be in my car five minutes ago.

If I skip around the Parkway and hit the 613 Bypass, I can get there. I need this shot. Everything is tied into it. The perfect picture lands the final, perfect grade and pretty much secures my acceptance into Trydan College's uber-elite art program. I'm already lined up to attend next fall, but if I don't secure a seat in that program, what's the point?

I jump the last two stairs, spin around the corner, and slam into an unexpected wall of muscle.

"Ems."

Grayson... Shit. "Hey, um, sorry."

I right myself, slinging the camera bag back on my shoulder, but I can't tear away from him. How did I not know he was here? As much as I've avoided him, now I don't want to go anywhere. Every second counts as the setting sun's light shifts over the thick forest cap. But his hands, his gaze. God, I'm not going anywhere to take that photo.

His hands move to my biceps, steadying me when I haven't realized I'm swaying. "You good?"

I nod. Yup, totally good. What's the question? What isn't the question? Because that thing where I can't think, breathe, function, move... I spiral into total Grayson reaction.

He lets me go and crosses muscular arms over an expansive chest. "You've been avoiding me."

"No. Not really." I cringe. "Maybe."

"Can't do that, Ems." He steps forward. His hand is on my side, backing me against the wall.

Oh, God. What if he kisses me again? I don't think I can keep upright. "I know. It's okay. I just..." Have no idea what to say or do.

"Want to tell me why?"

Ha. No way. "I was shopping after school this week."

"Haven't seen you at lunch, haven't seen you text, haven't seen you at all."

"Well, um..."

"We're still good for tomorrow?" His brows are up, but his smile is down. A concern mars his handsome face, and nodding is the only thing I can do to confirm Sadie Hawkins.

"See, this is the thing." He leans closer. "Me kissing you, you disappearing, that's my nightmare."

His nightmare?

He leans down. His face comes closer. "We've been tight since we were six. Don't let anything screw that up." The strongest guy I know shows a slice of vulnerability. "You don't know what you mean to me, Emma."

I... what? "Gray—"

His stomach touches mine. His hands move up and palm my cheeks. This guy could have *anyone* at school. But he's here in my house, saying this, doing this.

"I don't get it." My eyes sting. I can't explain why. Between the not breathing and the not thinking, tearing up couldn't come at a worst time. But my head's all over the place. My love, it's too strong, and if he ever knew... Whatever's burning between us, it's enough to make my daydreams seem like a possibility.

"What don't you get?" His thumbs caress my cheeks.

"This."

He pulls back and snags my hand. My camera bag drops off my shoulder, landing at the base of the stairs as he drags me back up. The closer we come to my room, the more my stinging eyes and breathing problems rage.

Then we're in my room. He shuts the door, and everything inside me tingles. My folks aren't home. My brother's in the basement. Just me and Gray behind my closed bedroom door.

"Sit down, Emma."

If he hadn't given me a little push, there's a chance I would've obeyed and dropped to the floor right there. Carefully, I sit on my bed, watching him pace, lost in silence. The twist on his face is confusing.

"Gray?"

He stops and turns to me. "You're the only one who can do that."

"Do what?" I whisper, uncertain of... everything.

"Stop my head. Freeze my mind. Bring me to another place. Or keep me where I need to be."

"Where's that?"

"I thought far away." He rubs his temples. "School's over in, what, three weeks?"

"Yeah."

"Then you're off to Trydan."

"In a few months." Biting my lip, I don't know where he's going with this. He hasn't said anything about college. I know he's had a couple of scouts talk to him at school, but discussions about the future—just like his home life—are off-limits. I know where, or if, he's going to college like I know what his bedroom looks like: I don't.

And he won't talk about it. I've tried more than once. His father is an asshole. That's all he's ever shared, but I picked up on that the few times I've seen his dad over the years. More than once, I've seen Grayson with bruises that he blames on football, though I've never seen Ryan like that.

Gray's home life is bad. I figured that out long ago when I started telling him stories. The future is what he avoids.

He crosses his thick arms, making his muscles flex. "This week fuckin' sucked."

I blink. "Why?"

"God," he growls. "Are you that blind?"

My eyes go wide. My heart slams in my chest. "No—"

He drops to his knees in front of my bed. His hands tear into my hair. His mouth finds mine, pulling me to him. This isn't a kiss. It's a pleading. No one's ever touched me like he does. It's hard and hot, and I didn't know kisses like this existed outside the movies.

"I'm sorry." I kiss him, bite him. God, I need him. "I'm scared of you."

He breaks from me, breathing hard. "*What*?"

"What if what you want isn't what I want?" I bite my lip. "What if I'm so far past..."

His arms wrap around me, and Gray pulls me with him as he crawls onto my bed. "Don't doubt this."

I nod, and his mouth finds my neck. Everything inside my body ignites. Deep in me, I'm dying for him, all lust-drunk and love-crazy. His hips flex, pushing his weight between my legs. My hands claw into his shirt, ripping to get under it and palm his skin, and when I do, he moans as my fingernails dig into his hot flesh.

But then he stops. I'm panting, my mouth open against his. His eyes freeze on mine, his breaths the mirror of mine. I feel his hard-on between my legs, thick and hard.

"You can't hide from me. You have no idea…" He blinks. "Promise me."

I nod.

"Good."

"Are you sure… about us?" Because I can't believe it. Wrapping my head around him and me, it's almost impossible. Very Cinderella—just a fairy tale come to life.

He grabs my hand and presses it to the bulge in his pants. I want to jerk away. I know my mouth's hanging open. That's so… so, oh my God. It's an asshole move, but it's not. It's… I don't know what it is. But it's forward, beyond anything I know how to comprehend.

"Emma." He lets my hand go. "You're adorable. And cute. Sweet. Better to me than anyone's ever been."

What does any of that have to do with us? "So is everybody else."

"Pretty doesn't begin to describe you, Ems. You're..."

"Awkward with a camera stuck to my face."

"The one I dream about."

My heart freezes. "Grayson..." *I love you.*

"You have no idea when it comes to what I think about you."

The sun has set. My room's light is turning a deep purple, and there's an urge to hug and hold him that has nothing to do with the kiss that just happened.

He leans over to kiss me. This time it's slow. He tastes like mint, and I'm mesmerized by the lazy roll of his mouth. Grayson holds my hip. His fingers flex, and his thumb scores back and forth over the slip of bare skin under my shirt. We could stay here for hours. Maybe we will.

His teeth tug my bottom lip. "I gotta run."

My chest is tight, and I crave his hands, his mouth everywhere. But everyone will be home soon, and my total inexperience is going to put me into a position where I want more than I know what to do about. "Okay."

One more kiss, and he leaves me on my back. "Bye, Ems."

"Bye." I kick my feet to the wall and wish Cherry was on the other side. Instead, I text her, expecting her to reply with something like, *go find that boy and jump him.* Maybe someday soon, I will.

CHAPTER FIVE

EMMA

Today, we killed the juniors in the powder-puff game. Football's no joke, and even though it was all fun and games, I'm sore. I swallow a couple of Tylenol before Grayson picks me up because nothing's slowing me down for tonight's Sadie Hawkins, not sore muscles or nervous stomach twinges or the excited anticipation of walking in on his arm, knowing there's more than a good chance his lips will be on mine sometime tonight.

The doorbell rings, and my stomach jumps.

"Gray's here." Mom made such a fuss when Ryan's date picked him up that maybe she's not having the same holy shit moment I am. Grayson used the doorbell? In what world does that happen? He just walks in. He may even have a key because I know he's been here when we haven't.

One last twirl before my mirror, and the blue dress seems smaller and tighter than anything I'm used to wearing. I can't explain how much I love it. My heart pounds, wondering what his reaction will be.

I fumble for my purse. Again, one more time, just in case, I spin in front of the mirror. Maybe this dress is too much? It's just a stupid Sadie Hawkins—

"Emma?" Mom's heels come closer.

Right. I can do this. He likes me. I love him. No pressure. Shit, shoot, shit... Okay.

I head to the stairs, each step closer to my big reveal, and I can't fight the giddy smile on my face. He's bringing out a part of me that I've always had but kept hidden.

As I stand at the top of the stairs, Mom stops mid-conversation with an unseen Grayson and gapes. "William," she calls to my dad. "Honey, come see Emma."

Dad's in the background, futzing with whatever he's doing. Neither Mom nor Dad would have expected this. It's just a dance with Gray. But it's so much more, and this dress announces it. At least in my mind it does.

As I descend the stairs, my eyes track to Grayson, and the desire on his face makes my chest feel tight. A nervous grin I can't hide crosses my face, and he steps forward. He's wearing a suit that makes him look like a movie star ready for the red carpet. His broad shoulders in the dark jacket are large but lean. The stark white shirt unbuttoned at the collar epitomizes sexy. Everything about him screams out of my league. He's just so... Grayson.

His lips part as he walks to me. "Wow."

One word. But the effect he has on me is nothing short of epic. Under his scrutiny, I'm redcarpet worthy alongside him. Words like pretty or beautiful, even sexy, don't begin to cover how he makes me feel. A dangerously chaste kiss lands on my cheek, and he breathes deep. "Hell of a dress."

Holy. Shit. And three days of non-stop shopping is now totally worth it. One of his hands grazes across my bare shoulder, and the need to throw myself against his hard body is unbearable.

Dad meanders into the room and glances me up and down. "Gorgeous, sweetie pie." Then he turns to Grayson and claps him on the back. "Keep an eye on her for me."

Dad chuckles and pulls Mom under his arm. They have no idea. I think they think that Grayson's my pity date and that I asked him because there's no one else I could-would-should ask. Dad's subtle warning isn't for Gray. It's for Gray to keep others away. Mom and Dad always said I didn't know how the world saw me. Maybe they were right. But it doesn't matter. Gray's the only one I care about.

When we leave my house, his large hand spans the small of my back. He has me close, and my stomach is on rotation, flip after flop. This feels like one of those chick flicks where I just know everything will come together in the end.

"I like you in a suit, Gray."

He tucks me into the passenger seat, crouches down, and catches my hand as I reach for my seatbelt. His hand is strong and confident. "I like you any way you come."

Then he pulls back to shut the door. I don't even know this guy anymore, but I can't get enough. Ten minutes later, we're at school and heading inside, his hand holding mine. Strings of lights sparkle overhead, glittering like stars and transforming the gym into something worth remembering.

When Gray told Kelly I'm his date, it never occurred to me that I'm actually going to *be* his date. Four years of high school, countless dances, and he's always been my dream guy. Probably everybody else's too.

I catch a glance of Ryan talking with his date, some floozy that surely gave him a BJ before they got here. That's what happens. People hook up. They hang out.

My stomach flutters. Dating doesn't really exist. People can be fuck buddies. Then after a couple of weeks, they're heartbroken or they're not, but they move on. At least that's how it seems to me. No one really *dates*. It's old and awkward. But Gray and me? It's been two weeks of nervous moments, hot kisses, and awesomeness. So whatever it's called, I love it.

Shifting in heels that I should never have worn, I scan right to left. It's a sea of dresses and suits. Couples who have been watching the dance floor are now looking at me. At *us*. The stares are like a chokehold.

"Gray..." I lean against him.

The whole gym sees me on his arm, hand in hand, when I realize that even *Gray* is looking at me. Blood rushes in my neck, screams in my ears. My lungs go tight, and that has nothing to do with the dress I poured myself into. He leans over and presses his lips to my temple. "Let them talk."

Ryan sees us, studies our handhold, and I can see him processing the Gray-me couple. After a few long seconds, my brother gives Grayson a chin lift and me a smile. It's the Ryan Kingsley stamp of approval.

Gray's lips drag across my forehead, and I sway into him. The whispers start as we walk farther in. Their eyes follow the football star-art nerd combo. They're used to seeing us like *us* over the years, not like this, arms connected, bodies touching. This is different. His fingers are intertwined with mine. He's so close and smells like clean, soapy heaven.

"People are looking at us."

His hand squeezes. "Good."

"Kelly Reynolds is drooling over you."

He laughs. "And every dude here's doing the same for you."

What? I bite my lip but lean into him. "Liar."

Gray whips me around, arms around my waist, backing me to the dance floor where everyone who isn't staring is dancing. The music is fast, the beat strong. But we're almost slow dancing, and the motion leaves me desperate and anxious, wanting more of him than I've had.

I corral all of my nerves and bravery into one giant question. "So is this some kind of boyfriend-girlfriend thing?"

He slows even though we are already moving at a swaying crawl. My throat tightens. This can't be good. Panic scares away the bravery, and my foolishness is debilitating.

With narrow eyes, he inches closer. "Is that what you want?"

Is he kidding me? I blink, afraid to give my answer. "I…"

I'm unsure how it's even possible, but his arms hold me closer. His breath touches my ear. "You could do so much better than me."

Laughing uncomfortably, I don't understand any of this. He wants me, or he doesn't. The hand holding and hugging isn't a move for a fuck buddy. It's all so genuine it hurts.

"Why say that, Gray?"

"Hm?"

"You're playing *you* down to *me*? I mean, it's *you*. Everyone in this gym would die to be me this second."

He chuckles. "I don't play me down."

"You do." It's like we see-saw who's confident and who's in disbelief. "You have everything."

"What I have is…" A lost, pained expression passes across his face. "We need to talk."

"Hey, you two—" Mr. Snyder, my junior year history teacher and one of Gray's coaches, taps my shoulder. "Give it some breathing room."

A hot blush crawls onto my cheeks. "Oh, yeah. Sorry"

Gray doesn't let go. "Just dancing, Coach."

Mr. Snyder's brows furrow, and he scowls at Gray. "*Of course*, Grayson. Some space please, Miss Kingsley."

What the heck is that attitude coming from his coach?

"She's fine. Right, Emma?"

"Yeah, of course."

"Not going to tell you again." Mr. Snyder's watching me, acting as if he's protecting me.

"But—"

"That's okay. We're out of here. C'mon." Grayson snags my hand, and I feel a hundred eyeballs follow us toward the gym door.

We've only been here a few minutes, but with his wanting to talk and my wanting to do anything but talk, I follow without question.

Mr. Snyder's steps are hot on our trail. "Once you leave, you can't re-enter."

"No prob." Grayson doesn't turn around.

"Wait," Mr. Snyder snaps.

I peer over my shoulder, slowing my date down.

My teacher's gaze drifts to our entwined hands. "Miss Kinglsey, do *you* want to stay here?"

My eyes peel back in surprise. "What? No."

Gray steps closer. "Coach—"

Mr. Snyder ignores him. "If you need a ride, Emma, I'm sure *your brother* or one of your friends can—"

"Nice. Thanks, Coach." Grayson scoffs, and the sarcasm rolls. "Let's go, Ems."

I nod, letting him pull me out the door. Another quick look over my shoulder, and Mr. Snyder's worry shakes me. Gray keeps me with him. We reach his car, and he sets me in it, shuts the door, and storms to the driver's seat. When he gets in, he slams the door and scowls out the windshield.

"What's... going on?" I'm lost. Everything warm and fuzzy is gone, which I hate.

He turns his head. "Really?"

"Uh, yeah."

"Shit, Ems." He throws his head back, and his laughter fills the car with an uneasiness that is lost on me.

"Gray, seriously. What was that?"

"That's everyone's concern for you with me, verbalized."

My forehead pinches. "I don't get it."

"You're like... innocent. And I'm not."

"No, I'm not."

He laughs. "You are, baby, and I'm the guy who can nail any chick in this school." He shakes his head. "Coach Snyder knows it."

Yup. I'm a virgin. *Everyone* probably assumes that. "Oh…"

"Yeah."

"He thinks… what, you're going to…" I cover my smile with my hands. "Defile me?" I want to be embarrassed that my teacher ran after me to pro-tect—what? —my honor. But can't. Not now. Not with Grayson. A giggle I can't stop bursts out.

"Defile?" His grin hitches to the side, and I see softness in his green eyes. "Something like that."

Again, I muster my bravery and hold it deep. Before I can think my thoughts through, my mouth's moving, and my heart's screaming. "What if a girl like me wants to be defiled?"

If I lose my virginity, it has to be to him. Right? Someone I love? Someone I want? Someone who's always been there and who I trust to never disappear?

The softness in his eyes disappears. "Don't say that."

"Oh." My face falls. Everything falls. He wants me, but not like that? Not that much?

His fingers catch my chin, turning me so that I face him. "Ems, nothing about you should ever be defiled."

I blink. "Okay."

Whatever word he wants to use, I'm ready. I don't know when or where, but I want Grayson Ford to be my first.

Really, I want him to be my only.

"It's just that the future is confusing. And sex is whatever, but sex with you... that's not. It's..." He shakes his head.

I shrug to hide my disappointment, completely heartbroken. What is this between us? And who knew *not* having sex was hurtful too?

Gray clears his throat. "Ems... It's the 'you and me' thing again. I'm..."

"You've never had a problem getting a date," I offer, jealous. "I certainly don't think you have a problem sleeping with—"

"Come on, Emma. Don't be like that. It's just that you are..."

I hate every second he doesn't finish that sentence.

"I'm a virgin." Tears burn my eyes. "That's it. It's because I'm a virgin."

CHAPTER SIX

GRAYSON

Virgin. My head drops, and I rub my temples, mumbling something along the lines of I can't say no to her anymore. Truth is, even I don't know what I'm saying. I'm trying not to beg, trying not to run, needing to touch her, taste her. But I let her words run through my head. Even if I can't offer Emma anything that she deserves, I can't say no. The girl's had my heart since before I knew it went missing.

"Gray?" she whispers.

I'm unable to give her a response. My mind reels. She wants us. I want us. I picture her naked, pressed against me, and I'm going to fall apart.

And to be her first... That's enough to make me wish I'd never touched another girl, that we were each other's firsts. It's selfish, but even if I'm gone, even if she's in college, living some incredible life one day, she'll have to remember me.

I turn the engine over and drive.

"Where we going?"

Some place I can have her alone, look into her eyes, and run my hands all over her. Blood thumps in my chest. "My place."

"Your place?"

I should expect the shock in her voice. How many years have I known her, and how often has she been over? Never. I think maybe she's always known that it's not a good place, that it's my hell. But Pops has been on a bender for a few days already, and he hasn't been home. Times like this, he won't show up for a week, maybe two, and those spells of abandonment are the happiest memories I have.

Until now.

"Yeah." Turning toward her, I catch her eyes. "You good with that?"

However she wants to take that, I mean it. Is she good with me and her? Is she good with a shitty trailer?

"I'm good as long as I'm with you." Her fingers tangle with mine as I drive away from school.

God, I love her so much that my heart aches.

We drive down Route 6 and hit the entrance for my place. It's on a weedy plot, and the metal rust-bucket box isn't any better inside. But it's home, and tonight, it's ours.

Killing the engine, I give her a nod and jump out to grab her door. Emma's an angel, everything perfect and right and innocent in the world with buttery blonde hair and brown eyes so light they twinkle in the moonlight. She blinks with a nervous hesitation that brings me to my knees.

I take her hand in mine and squeeze, tugging her and that sinful dress beside me. "The place isn't much to look at. But we'll be alone."

"Really?"

The sweetness in her voice cuts straight through me. I've fucked, I've screwed, but this... this isn't anything like I've gone near before. My heart picks up its pace. My throat tightens, and something powerful bleeds through me.

After we push through the door and I hit a light and bring her down the short hall, I can tell her "really." But until she's in my room, in my bed, it won't feel real.

Emma drops her hand from mine and locks her arm around my waist. We push through my door, and she leans against me so I can hold her close. Short, quick bursts of breaths fall from her lips, and I'm suddenly so hard I hurt. Her hands run up my chest, and the longer she touches me, the more sure she seems.

"This is what you want, baby?" And I pray that she says yes, that she didn't see the crap trailer and remember that I'm a nobody who hides shitty circumstances well.

"Yes." She nods. "More than anything."

That's all I need. Our lips lock. I find the zipper on the back of her dress and drag it down. It hangs loose, and for as many times as I've imagined her naked, I'm barely able to control my hands slipping behind the fabric to touch bare skin.

Her hands freeze on the buttons on my shirt. Where she was soft and hot, she's gone rigid in my arms.

Hugging her tight, I crush her hands between us. "Ems? You good?"

"I…" She bites her lip nervously. "Don't know what I'm doing."

So sweet. God, so sweet. "Yeah, you do. Whatever you want, you do."

She catches my eyes, and I see it then: the curiosity and hunger, the desperate want both of us failed to ignore.

"Yeah? Just… take what I want?"

"Absolutely."

I can promise her the world, promise to take care of her, make her feel amazing, but that's not what she needs. Just a push of confidence is all she wants, something she thinks I have in spades. My lips touch her forehead, her cheeks. My fingers trace the contours of her back, skimming the slope of her spine. Shivers erupt under my touch, and she shimmies and lets the dress fall to the ground. Emma Kingsley is standing in my bedroom in lingerie and high heels. "Christ."

There's nothing to do but drop to my knees and love her. My mouth finds her belly, and as I swirl my tongue over her stomach, I unbutton my shirt and shrug it off.

"I like this." Her fingers trail my bare shoulders, sliding up and into my hair. Then she reaches behind to unclasp her bra. "So much."

Breasts bared to me, she has no idea, no fuckin' clue how much I like this too, how I could come right now. "You okay?"

She nods and sighs loud enough that I feel it in my groin.

"Good." My chest is tight. I hook her arms, hold her to me, and pull us down, bare chest to bare chest.

"More than okay." Her hands rub my back, my biceps. Her hips flex for mine. Her kisses run deeper, stronger. The girl tests her teeth on me, scraping softly enough I want to pay attention but hard enough I'll just enjoy the damn feel of it.

"Fuck, I like that, Ems."

The smile on her face, the way she comes alive, means tonight's meant to be.

She looks away. "So do you have condoms or whatever, 'cause I'm not..."

"Yeah." But I have all night with her. No way could I rush this. "We'll get there."

"Promise?" Her eyes are back on me, confidence on fire, arousal making her demanding.

I nod. "But we've got a checklist first."

"We do?" She laughs.

Nodding again, I run my fingertips from her chin to the top of her chest. "I'm going to kiss you here." Then lower over the swell of her breast, teasing the nipple. "Here again." Then palm the mound between her legs. "Then here."

She sucks in a breath. "Gray."

"Unless you don't want me to."

Her eyes go wide. "I do." Her face turns serious. "Thank you."

"What for?"

"The best night of my life."

Shit. I'm done. I can't stay off of her. With every kiss and touch, she laughs, whispers, and moans. It's a deadly combination, and the sounds are mine to keep. This night, it's the best I'll ever have too.

Her fingernails bite into my flesh as my fingers slide beneath her panties. She moves against me, and I'm going to lose myself if she keeps that up. But God, I want her too. I want to see her come. I want to watch it and own it, to know I did that, gave that to her.

"Grayson." Her breaths are ragged, and even as I work my fingers between her legs, I'm flexing my hips to her side. "Gray... God..."

Her body clenches, her thighs press together, she juts her hips up, and I feel her climax down to my soul. It's the only thing I can focus on. Hell, the world can stop spinning and I wouldn't notice—

A dark, nasty cackle comes from the hall. I jump. Emma jumps.

"Finally nailing that tart. That's my boy," Pops snarls from the dim hallway.

A chill freezes over us, and he staggers into my room.

"Oh, God," Emma's embarrassed cry shreds me, and for a snap of a second, I don't know what to do. Protect her and kill him. I'm angrier than I can fathom. But what the fuck did I think would happen? Nothing good comes in this trailer. Nothing. Ever.

"First time with this one?" Pops falters after a bad step, and a cigarette tucked behind his ear falls to the floor.

"What the fuck?" I growl. Never do I say a word. Never do I handle my shit with him. I'm stronger, bigger, more of a man than he'll ever be, but because I ruined his life, I've taken his crap, his attacks, the vulgar nature of his existence.

Until now.

He hurt the one person who saves me. I toss my covers over her but stare at him. "Get out!"

He steps closer, cigarette and whiskey stench rolling off of him. He claps off-cadence, chuckling to himself like I'm the night's entertainment. "Don't let me stop you."

Jesus. The pressure in my head nears dangerous levels, but I swallow away my reaction. That doesn't mean I haven't come up with a list of what should happen. Maim. Kill. Bury. "Out."

"You're all the time eye-fuckin' my women." Pops sways in the middle of the room, and I'm on my feet. "Think you're big man." He coughs and slurs. "Think you can take from me, and I can't take from you."

I snag her dress from the floor and toss it on the bed. "Get dressed, Ems. Take my car. Go. I'll—"

Pops' drunken right hook catches me on the back of the head. I didn't see it coming and don't feel it now. All I can process is the look of complete disgust on her face.

I turn to the greasy-haired bastard. "Don't do this now."

Like the sleaze he is, Pops laughs. "Years, you don't got shit to say. Get a girl in your bed, you're a big dick with a motor mouth."

"Emma, come on. Take my car—" He shoves me. Humiliation curls deep in my gut. I know I deserve his anger but not like this. Not in front of Emma. I spin to him. "Enough!"

He cough-laughs and throws a fist. I dodge it like all the others I could've dodged my whole life but didn't. His drunken eyes go wide. His mouth parts enough to show he didn't expect to miss. I never move. But tonight I do because Emma's frozen in place.

Her eyes say everything's changed, that maybe she's disappointed or disgusted. Maybe she now knows I live here with him on this side of town for a reason. Whatever's in her mind, I'm no longer what she knows. Embarrassed fear grips me.

"Emma." I reach for her, and she jolts back to reality.

"Shit." She grabs her dress, clutching it to her chest, and tears slide down her cheeks. "Shit, shoot, shit."

Fiery anger builds in my chest. It's red, hot, and rabid. I can't see, can't breathe, and I growl toward Pops. "Get out. Get the fuck out."

He rushes me, hands outstretched. Enough. Fuck him. I'm done. As his fists start their drunken descent, I unleash years of fury. A roar blasts from deep within me. My blows strike with scary accuracy. Head shot. Gut shot. Right hook, left hook. Each lands with impact. Vengeance takes over my limbs. I'm not thinking or feeling. Only doing.

I grab him and slam us against the wall, my hands around his neck. One. Two. Three. And he's done. Out. I let go, and he drops, crumpling on the ground, and I don't give a shit. A cold sweat's taken over my body, and my lungs pound. Adrenaline fueled me, but now I'm starved for oxygen, for sanity.

I glance over at my bed. Emma's tears flow freely. Her bottom lip quivers as she stares at Pops, and then eyes track back to mine.

Fuck me. My hands go clammy. My throat closes up. Adrenaline abates, letting my throbbing head and racing blood slow. Never in my eighteen years have I felt her scrutiny. Never. But now, there it is. Pity. Fright. Confusion.

Unsteadily, she stands, dressing without looking at me. She presses her lips together. "Are you okay?"

I nod, humiliation back, making me angry all over again. This is my life. That is my dad. This is where I live, where I'm trapped. As much as I hide from it at school, *this is me*. And I can't escape.

I look down at Pops, still out. Tonight was supposed to be perfect, the best night ever.

"I have to go." She slides off the bed.

My head drops. "I know…"

"This is what happens. Isn't it, Gray? The football bruises that Ryan never has. The—"

"Don't." I shake my head. I can't let her go there because *I* can't go there. "Forget it." But she deserves as much of the truth as I can stomach. "I've never hit him back before." I rub my temples, still studying the carpet. "Never."

She gasps the softest, saddest breath. "Really?"

Ha. There's a fucked-up logic I could never explain.

"You're twice his size. Why?" She bites her bottom lip. "It doesn't matter. You don't have to—"

"Stop." She's pitying me. God, fuck me, she's trying to map out some life solution for me. "You have to get out." I choke on the shame. "Please. He wasn't supposed to be here."

"I'm so sorry." Her shoulders slump, and her chin's down.

Slowly, I shift and shake my head, a complete disgrace. "Take my car home. Give Ryan the key. We'll just forget tonight…" Forget us because I'll never be able to face her again. All over, I've gone from angry to embarrassed.

Pops stirs on the floor. I'm not going to be here when he wakes up, and neither is she. "Go, Ems."

Tears brim in her eyes. We're breaking apart before we ever started. Part of me wants to beg her to forget this side of me. Another part wants to rejoice that someone knows how deeply I hurt, but I shake my head. "It's not supposed to be like this. It's…"

I can't sugarcoat an explanation. I grab my keys, force them into her hand, then drag Emma to the front door of the trailer I've never been able to escape.

"Please don't—"

"Just go."

She nods and obeys, leaving in silence. The front door slaps shut, and I punch the wall. I'm angry. Heartbroken. Devastated. And completely alone.

CHAPTER SEVEN

GRAYSON

Only a few lights shine down, and sweat beads down my back. I couldn't stay home but had nowhere to go except here, the batting cages where the owner lets me have access anytime day or night. The lights are always on and the gate is always open. It's just me, the ball, and the bat pushing toward midnight.

It's been hours since Emma left my place and I grabbed the keys to Pops's truck. If I stop pushing myself, I'll have to deal with the fallout from tonight. Pops is gonna kill me. He would even if I hadn't borrowed his truck while he was sawing Zs on the floor. Emma's never going to see me the same way. And me. If I look in a damn mirror, I'll be sick. I wanted to leave the second school's over. Running away from my past is an alright way to go once everyone else heads to college. But now I need a plan.

Clicks pop from down range, and the mechanical arm launches another baseball toward me. I'm past even a decent form. I'm exhausted. My muscles scream. One ball after the next, I can't stop swinging, sick over the future, knowing that I had the world fooled until tonight.

Finally nailing that tart. Pops's words reverberate in my head. Another ball flies. Swinging, I embrace the burn in my back, the ache in my arms. A satisfying crack echoes as it flies, another home run that doesn't go anywhere.

The clicks and pops signal another one inbound.

I need to talk to Ryan. He always trusted me with Emma, would never have a problem with me being with her. There's no way he'd think I could hurt her. Because I couldn't. *I can't.* But I did. Fuck me, I did.

The Kingsleys are the only family I've had, even if they aren't really mine. I shake my head, grinding my hands on the grip. A ball flies. Crack. Another one heading for the fence. I should text Ryan. If Emma showed up at home in tears with my car, he's gonna have a problem with me. Their parents will too. My stomach drops. None of that matters, though, not when she's been the only thing that's allowed me to survive, and now she's gone.

All because of Pops. And Mom. Shit, what would my mom do? What would she think? Why couldn't this have been better for her? For us? My mind churns.

Just another one. I can see her face. Vividly. Even when I was a kid, her perfect make-up confused me. She was so pretty. So lost. I want to throw up. God, I can't shake her eyes on me in my memories. I'm going fuckin' nuts. Everyone's in my head: Pops, Ryan, and now Mom. *Just another one, honey. Another minute, Grayson. It'll be okay. It'll always be okay with another one.*

Fuck! It's not okay. It was never okay. Why did she burden me with this? Rage blinds me, and I throw the bat, screaming into the night. The clink and clash of it hitting the fence does nothing to reduce the pounding in my head. I tear my hands into my hair, and it's too short, too tight to grab. I'm seconds away from collapsing, from a complete nervous breakdown.

"Take a breath, son."

Whirling around, I'm sweat-drenched and face-to-face with our ROTC adviser, Marcus Waylon. "What're you doing here?"

"Chaperoning that dance, saw the shit with Snyder. Then I drive by, and you're out here, alone?" He clucks his tongue. "Had to pull in."

Waylon isn't much older than me. He maybe graduated a few years ago. He didn't do college.

Did do the military. He's here not because he wants to be anywhere near this side of the United States, but because he's on Uncle Sam's payroll, and they put him here in Virginia as an Army recruiter.

He walks closer. I blink, searching for words, gasping for breaths. Shit knows what he must think about me right now. I flex my aching fingers. "What'd you want, sir?"

He takes another step closer and glares. "Better question, Ford, is what're you doing?"

Trying to outrun my nightmares, hide from my pain. I take a deep breath. My pulse is thumping in my temples, my neck. Trying to slow my heart rate, I make him wait a minute. "Working out. Hitting the cages."

"Baseball season's over." Waylon's arms cross. "Try again."

Avoiding the two people I can't control, Pops and Emma. "Blowing off steam."

He nods. "I talked to Coach. He said—"

C'mon on already. What is it with tonight? "That prick? Seriously. That goddamn prick thinks—"

"You don't know what he thinks." Waylon grabs and tosses my ignored bottle of water.

I catch it and guzzle half, thinking of how both Snyder and Waylon must think of me. I know what the world sees. I let them see it: good looks, good grades, good at sports. Package trifecta. I get it. But, man, they're wrong. Everyone's wrong. "Coach thinks Emma isn't—"

"I know what's going on with you at home."

Well, fuck me. My hand crushes the plastic bottle. "Yeah. Right." I scuff my shoe into the dirt. "Of course, you do."

Waylon ignores my attitude. "It's easy enough to figure out once you get past all your cocky bravado."

"Easy. Right." First Snyder, now Waylon, both guys I would've thought would be on my side. I'm just as smart as Pops thinks I am. All the voices, doubts, memories, they start to choke me again. Everyone's in my head. Pops. Emma. Ryan. Mom. Snyder. Waylon. It's too much. My sore fingers knead my neck, locking in my hair. I can't catch my breath. The pressure's too much on my lungs. In my head. My throat's closing up.

"Take a breath." Waylon steps closer. "Calm down."

Shit, I can't calm down, can't make it stop. "I need to get out of here."

"Where you going to go?"

Where am I going tonight? Not home. Not the Kingsleys', not after everything with Emma. My chest hurts again. A virgin. She's *my* virgin. She's my world, my heart.

I can't believe how things fell apart. I ruined it—ruined us—and I'm not even sure I can survive the next ten minutes, let alone the rest of school. Emma's the only thing that saves me. Shit, I can't breathe. That look on her face? My dream, my savior, I've lost her tonight, and my heart's going to explode.

A hand claps on my back. I startle, my head shoots up and I'm dizzy with panic.

Waylon's face is serious. "Let's go."

That's all he says before he turns and heads towards the parking lot. I have no reason to go with him, none to stay at the batting cages, and nowhere else to go. A lonely exhaustion hugs me, and unable to see anything but pain, humiliation, and desperation, I follow.

CHAPTER EIGHT

EMMA

Cherry: *You sure you're good?*

That's the fifth text message from Cherry to-day. I'd spilled my guts when she came in for graduation. We spent a whole weekend bitching about boys, enough to scare Ryan away from all questions about where Grayson has been, but even my brother's caught on, giving the occa-sional *it's-okay* grin.

After Cherry went back to college, she started a daily text message campaign. Her goal was to ready me for today: D-day. Or rather B-week. Beach week.

In our town, every senior takes the week after graduation, teams up with their friends, and rents a house for a week of celebration. A few of us rented a beach house. My small group obviously includes Grayson, so for the fifth time today, I lie and text Cherry back.

Emma: *Doing awesome. Seriously, no worries.*

It takes her two seconds to call me out on it.

Cherry: *Liar. Call me if you need me. xx*

Yeah, I need her in a major way, but what am I going to do? Have my big sister come home and bunk with me? Besides, I don't want her around Grayson. She's got a heart like mine, and she's a fixer, a planner, and after what I confided in her, she wants to show up at Grayson's place and do something about his dad.

The problem, we decided, is that he's eighteen. He could leave. But leave what? Go where? If he won't talk to me, then I'm left to my own thoughts, which haven't been great. I groan. I'm so confused.

"Hey, hon?" Mom knocks softly and walks in. She's had an eye on me for the last few weeks, and I'm pretty sure that Cherry ratted me out after graduation. Not that she told Mom I offered up myself in bed, but I'm sure Mom knows there was a falling out between me and Gray.

It's been weeks since the Sadie Hawkins disaster. Gray can do his thing, and I'll do mine. He hasn't been to lunch. He hasn't returned a phone call or text, nothing online. Nothing. I almost caught him when I came out of the school dark-room, but he ditched down a hall right when the bell rang, and I was stuck staring after him and holding a handful of photography supplies.

Gray's still hanging with everyone *but* me *and* still going to the beach house. I'm not sure what to do, especially on the ride out there with Ryan and Gray. How should I act? What do I say? Maybe ignore it all? Whatever I do, it won't mat-ter. My heart's still bleeding. I lost him, and it hasn't made me love him any less.

Judging by the pictures from the rental site, there's a chance it will be just like school. We'll never bump into each other, given how big that house is. I could always follow him around like some PI ninja, but that's pathetic, just like how I feel.

Ugh, I stifle a groan and turn to Mom. "Hey."

"Have you talked to Ryan this morning?"

"No." I shake my head. "What's up?"

"He was up all night, sick."

My eyebrows rise. "What?"

She leans against the door jam. "I think he has food poisoning, but either way, he's going to miss the first day or two of beach week."

Shit, shoot, shit. Nervous excitement at the thought of a car ride alone with Grayson rolls through me. It's at my brother's expense, which kinda makes me an awful person. "Yeah, okay."

Maybe Ryan's hungover from his spiral of post-grad partying. Mom leaves, and I grab my phone. After a few minutes of texting Ryan to no avail, I roll out of bed and knock on his door.

No answer, so I nudge open the door. He doesn't seem hungover, just sleepy. But he sounds like shit, croaky and gross.

"Don't come in here, Emma." He pulls the pillow over his head.

"No prob." Germs aren't my thing. I would bathe in hand sanitizer if I could. Getting sick is a nightmare.

Okay. Alright. Shit. Okay. What do I do? We're supposed to leave, like... right now.

"Have fun." He coughs. "Catch up with you guys soon as I can."

If Ryan, Grayson, and I are supposed to ride together, does that mean now it's just Gray and me? I bite my lip. It seems benign enough except my pulse thumps. But would Gray ride with just me?

Of course he would. Right? He might be avoiding me, but he's not an asshole.

Gray's gotta be mature enough to sit in a car and, at the very least, ignore me for a couple of hours. What if I can't handle the close quarters alone with him? Maybe I should call up Courtney or Melanie and ride with them, just to save everyone an awful few hours. Time is ticking and—

"Emma," Mom calls from downstairs.

My stomach leaps into my throat. It's go time. Grayson must be here already. I head that way, stopping on the final step, nerves firing. *Please don't let him leave when he finds out Ryan won't join us.* I'm not sure I could handle such direct avoidance.

"Emma, get down here, hon. Gray's—" She rounds the corner and steps toward me, her face confused. "Hey, Gray's here."

I peek over Mom's shoulder, and he's inching toward the door. My world spins just seeing him. He's beautiful, handsome, so tall and strong. I think the last few months have changed him from a boy to more of a man. He's just so... Gray.

Knowing his lips had been on mine and why he won't talk to me makes my soul ache. Down to the very base of my body, I hurt. I miss him. Forget that I love him and that I want to hold him. I need him with a desperation I can't explain, and I want him to know that what happened with his dad, it's unacceptable, but it's not worth losing us over.

"Emma?" Mom gives me a onceover. It's like she can sense something's off but can't put two and two together. Maybe I was wrong about Cherry giving her any gossipy details.

Here goes nothing. "Hey, Gray."

He turns, and piercing green eyes draw me to him. "Ems."

The only word I've heard from him in weeks and it has to be Ems. I'm lightheaded.

"Alright, you two." Mom gives me a hug. "Have fun. Give me kisses, Emma."

I kiss her cheek, but my brow drops as I find the courage to tell him he's stuck with me. "Oh, um. Ryan's riding out later."

Grayson's jaw flexes. "Right. That's what your mom said." He shoves his hands in his pockets, his giant shoulders hulking. But his eyes still hold mine. "Okay, let's go."

His obvious discomfort around me is painful. I can't do this. Maybe this was a bad idea, riding with him. "Ya know… I'll hitch a ride. Or drive myself."

Mom laughs. "You're not driving yourself to the beach, Emma. My God. Grayson, her bag is in the mudroom. You two need anything? You're good on cash? Dad shoved another couple twenties in your bag after he said bye this morning."

Numbly, I can't think of an argument that doesn't make me sound pathetic. I stare at the hardwood floor. Grayson passes me, and I hear him grab my bag. When he walks by, my bag thrown over his shoulder, his soapy scent makes my mouth water and my eyes tear. I want that so bad. I want him. So much. So pathetic.

At my door, he turns. "You need anything else?"

Um... Yeah. You. Back to normal with me. But really, I do need my purse and toiletry bag. "Give me a minute."

I run upstairs, grab my crap, and text Cherry.

Emma: *Things are more complicated. But I'll survive. Call you later.*

She doesn't ping me back, and there's no option but to get into Gray's car. Actually, there are a million options. The truth is, I'm hurting so much, missing him even more, and I refuse to miss a chance to sit next to him, even if it's in uncomfortable silence, for the next few hours.

"Bye, Mom."

From somewhere, she shouts back, and then I'm out the door to meet him at his car. Each nervous step feels heavier than the next, and by the time my hand touches the door handle, I'm concerned I'll puke from nerves. So much for saving the friendship.

"Hey," he mumbles.

"Hey." I climb in and trap myself next to him. Delicious insanity. I want to hug him, hold him, kiss him, scream at him, plead for words, beg for a conversation. But I just buckle my seatbelt.

He backs out. It's a three-hour drive to the beach. When we show up, we won't be alone. Courtney and Melanie left this morning. Trevor and James arrived last night. Our drive out is my only chance at... what? Everything.

My bravery is pooling again, despite our awkward silence. I bite my lips to keep quiet, but I know it won't work.

We merge onto the highway. His overwhelming presence fills his car, and when I take in his broad shoulders and strong jaw, it's more than my broken mind can handle. The thing about being heartbroken is that I'm so ruined that I don't care if it happens again. I'm blinded by love. Blinded by heartbreak. Just... blind when it comes to him. I can't see anything past how I feel.

"You okay over there?" His voice interrupts my thoughts.

"What?"

"You're..." His hand flexes on the steering wheel. "Growling or something."

"I didn't growl."

He changes lanes, looking more at me than his blind spot. "So what was that?"

"I'm just...not okay. I want to scream. Or cry. Probably both. Because of you."

He rubs a hand over his face and into his hair.

If it wouldn't kill us on the highway, I would shake him. First, because my hands would be on him again, and it would be temporary heaven. But second, isn't it possible to rattle someone so hard that whatever is wrong with them—with us—slips away? "You told me I can't hide from you. You made me promise I wouldn't avoid you, Gray. *Promise*."

"Yeah, I know," he mumbles.

"What is it, a double standard?"

The radio station comes back from commercial, and his thumbs beat on the steering wheel. "You wouldn't understand, and I can't explain it."

He turns the music up. Riding with him was an awful idea, and now I can't breathe. My skin crawls. The seatbelt chokes me, and the air conditioning is blowing full blast, but it won't take the edge off the heat eating me alive.

"Everything was awesome. It was... perfect. And when—"

"Drop it, Ems. I can't talk to you about it."

My fingernails bite into my palms as I ball my fists in my lap. "Try me. Talk to me. Just say anything."

"I can't."

"Damn it, Gray. *Try!*"

Surprised, he turns his head. His eyes stay with me like we're not flying down the road. "Ems—"

"Stop with the Ems. Stops with *everything*," I scream. "Stop what's wrong. Stop it, stop it."

"Jesus, Emma, calm down. I'm not doing anything."

"Except you are." My body curls in on itself, and my head shakes. The sadness and loss is overwhelming. I just ache. My stuttering breaths fall ragged between my lips. A tear slips free.

"It's for the best—"

"I don't believe you." The guy who made me feel like I was so much more than some art nerd who happened to be his friend—that guy held me, kissed me. He made me want to give all of me to him.

"You'd never understand." His hand reaches over to find mine, and it sends a strike of lightning straight to my heart. "It's always been about you."

My eyes sink shut, and my mind spins. He's driving with his left hand. His right hand firmly holds my tight fist. His fingers flex and squeeze like he's trying to tell me something. I don't get it. But I do feel it.

I don't know why he runs from me, but I swear we're not over. He can fight, but if there's one gift he's given me over the past few weeks, or maybe even the years we've been building to this point, it's this car ride.

I take my other hand and clasp it over his, sandwiching our hands. Gray lets out a slow breath, and I hope that he sees we're not lost. Not yet. He's running, and I'll stop him. Save him. Grayson's the strongest guy I know, but right now, it feels like I'm holding him afloat.

"Emma, I did something that I can't get out of."

I swallow and wonder if this has to do with his dad or something else. "Okay."

"And I keep pretending if I don't know it's coming, maybe it won't happen."

Kind of like how I'm not thinking about Trydan. When the fall semester starts, I won't see him every day. It isn't that far away. Being a couple of states over isn't that big of a deal unless he asks me to stay, and then it would be... a yes?

Would I give up school and the photography program for Grayson?

Yeah. No question.

Everyone would call me foolish. They'd say I'm too young, that love doesn't come this quickly. But no one would know how long it's been or how deeply I love.

"You can tell me anything. I'll do anything. For you." For us...

He clears his throat. "That's what I'm afraid of." His hand squeezes mine. "Let's pretend next week isn't coming. Deal?"

I just swore I'd do anything for him. Of course he knows my answer. "Deal."

But already, I'm trying to map out my plan on how to make 'us' a 'we.'

CHAPTER NINE

EMMA

The beach house is rowdy. The guys are here. Ryan finally made it, and Trevor and James are a complete headache. Courtney and Melanie are gossiping, maybe—probably—about me. Ryan's had his eye on Gray, who's not kept his hands off of me, which earned me a quick conversation about Gray being both our friend, that he's the good guy we've always known, and that if something's going to happen while we're all here, Ryan wouldn't surprised.

Okay... Apparently, my brother missed the last few weeks of me moping around but seems totally honed in on the smile I can't hide now. But Ryan's right, and Gray and I are moving to a good place as beach week ticks on.

On day one, the heaviness of the car ride left us both fatigued. When everyone went out that night, we stayed in. Movies on the couch. We started on opposite ends, but by the time the credits rolled, I'd fallen asleep with my head in Gray's lap, his hand lazily toying with my hair.

What had happened between us weeks ago hovered somewhere between healing and ignored.

On day two, we were at the beach all day. Volleyball and games of chicken in the ocean. No one else went up on Gray's shoulders. They didn't try, so he didn't have to say no. We were connected at the hip except when I was squealing and screaming in the water, sitting high on his neck. His hands held my calves. His thumbs trailed my skin. And even with a million people around and freezing cold Atlantic Ocean water spraying us, my skin burned from his touch.

My Gray was coming back. The future wasn't in his head, and his eyes were only on me. I loved it. Loved him. God, so much.

On day three, I laid on the beach with the girls. They had twenty questions about us, none of which I would answer, mostly because I didn't know. But I didn't miss his glances when I lounged out of his reach with the girls. They were long and lazy. Ryan, Trevor, and James gave him some hell, to which he replied with a laughing middle finger. The guys backed off, the girls swooned, and I melted any time Grayson came near.

And that brings us to now, to my eyes tracking his beautiful body. For the better part of several days, he's only worn board shorts. Every sexy muscle is on display. I'd known for the last few months that Gray had been slamming extra workouts before and after school. I'm reaping the benefits. Ryan, Trevor, and James look fine. They take care of themselves. But Grayson Ford looks like a beach god. A couple of days' worth of sun has kissed him, and he's beyond words. But no lines have been crossed, no amazing conse-quences of our unacknowledged flirting. Even though we've been side-by-side nonstop, that's all it's been.

I'm done.

And I think he's done.

Each day, his eyes stay on me longer. His hands touch more boldly. Our laughs are too loud, our gazes too deep. If he doesn't kiss me soon, there's a very good chance I will implode. Just ka-blamy.

"We're gonna grill out. Heading to the store for steaks, beer, and whatever else," Ryan shouts from the front door. "Anyone coming, let's go."

Courtney and Melanie push past hi; the guys do too. It's just Gray and me waiting.

"You going?" I ask.

He steps closer, not answering. His hair is damp, having just showered, and sticking with his beach week uniform, he's back in shorts that hang dangerously low on his hips. I swallow, trying to ignore the V where his stomach muscles lead to his hipbones. But I can't. My eyes slide over him, and there is a distinct bulge in his dark shorts that can't be missed. The thumping of my pulse begins in my neck.

"Gray—"

The front door closes behind Ryan, and Grayson's on me. My body sings. His mouth takes mine. The kiss is rough, his possessive hands are greedy, and he's breathing like *I'm* breathing.

My bikini allows our bare stomachs to touch, and it sends me into carnal overdrive. All my senses are alive and infused with him. Sexy sounds make me purr. His lips devour mine and have me crawling and clinging to him. I let go of my hesitations and live in the moment, grasping his thick biceps.

Gray's hands run roughly over me. He palms and squeezes my breasts before he slides up and tears his fingers into my hair. Using the wall for leverage, I hook my legs around his hips, and he grabs my thighs, holding me in place.

"We're okay?" he growls against my neck.

"Yes…" I'm nodding into his kiss, arching into his mouth.

"Fuck me, I missed you."

I'm nodding more, hanging onto him for everything I've got. "You have no idea." Tears well in my eyes, and what started hot and hungry slows.

He senses me, knows me so well. Gray cups my cheeks, pushing me inches away. His eyes bore into me, removing every vulnerable layer I have. "You're all that's right in my head. You get that?"

No. Not a chance. "I'm whatever you need."

He nods. His lips dance over mine. He tastes so familiar, smells like my greatest weakness. How does he have the whole world fooled?

"Emma, no joke. If I didn't have you, I'd—" He shakes his head. "I need you, always have, in a way you'll never know."

"But I want to."

His eyes close tight. "No. You don't."

Hugging my body to his, I want to meld together. "Whatever's in your head, I wish you could trust me with it."

Placing a soft kiss to my temple, he sighs. "You want to know about Pops?"

I nod.

"Baby, it's dark and dangerous, and I don't think you could ever forgive me, ever be with the kind of person I am."

My heart squeezes. "Grayson, I will take you however you come. Don't you get that?"

"I deserve everything he's thrown at me. But that night? In front of you? I couldn't see straight, couldn't think." He closes his eyes, breathes deeply, then his green eyes open. "Haven't seen Pops since that night."

"He's just... gone?"

Grayson nods. "He has his reasons for hating me... but the look on your face. He hurt you, Emma, and I attacked just like he does. Fuck me, I'm not him and don't want you to think of me like that."

"I don't."

"I saw it in your eyes. You didn't want me, and I didn't blame you. But damn it, that hurt."

I kiss him, lightly at first, then stronger. "I want you in every way. Trust me. Believe me." My lips press to his again, and I kiss him hard, deep, needing to show him that there's nothing he can say that will make me walk away.

"Believe you." He clasps my face, holding my mouth to his. The kiss is intense. Consuming. I can't breathe, and I don't care. I just need him.

A noise outside tears us apart.

Ryan's car has pulled up to the beach house, and everyone is piling out. I'm panting. He's flushed. My lips feel swollen. My nipples are painfully hard and visibly outlined in my bikini top.

"Shit." Grayson's grip flexes. "You good for a minute?"

What does that even mean? I nod, slowing my breaths on purpose. "Yeah."

Grayson and his erection move to a kitchen chair, and I fumble, making sure my bathing suit is where it should be. It's not, and I fix it right as Courtney and Melanie walk in the door, their mouths moving a mile a minute, jabbering about whatever, with arms full of grocery bags. The guys are behind them with a case of beer—which means Ryan's priceless ID worked yet again— and a bag of charcoal for the grill.

One stare from Melanie, and I know I'm busted. Twenty seconds ago, I couldn't breathe. Of course it would be obvious that *something* was happening. She bursts out in giggles, raising a knowing eyebrow. It sets off a chain reaction with Courtney.

"Christ, man. The kitchen?" Ryan mumbles but has nothing more to say.

Grayson ignores them, stands to grab my hand, and tugs. "Let's go."

He wastes no time in showing us to the room he's sharing with Ryan, and he slides the lock on the door. I bite my lip, unsteady under Gray's intense stare.

"What are we doing?" I whisper.

"Ignoring the future."

My heart falls and jumps. Again with his fear of tomorrow, but does that mean he'll give me what I want?

"I'm not going to sleep with you, Emma. Not here. Like this. Not... now."

"Okay." Good. This isn't how I want it anyway, in some room he shares with my brother after we were basically caught making out. Nothing romantic about that. And I want it all: the future, the man, the feelings, and the emotion.

"But I am going to memorize every inch of your body."

Holy crap, I can't even begin to process what that will entail. The way he said it was predatory, and even as I stare, turned on and disillusioned, the timber of his voice crawls through me, sliding down my spine.

"Lie down, Ems."

And carefully, nervously, I do. When he sits beside me, the bed dips. He's by my ankles, and I'm lying stick straight. Again, my breaths fall faster just because of him, and it's so obvious on my back in my bathing suit. Not much to hide behind.

But he looms over me with his giant, tan shoulders beautifully within reach. The definition of his chest is scarily sharp.

We watch each other until I realize that I'm no longer stiff and straight but relaxed, loose, and aroused. His hand picks up my right foot. It tickles, and I twitch, which makes him smile.

"Easy, baby."

Baby. My heart stops. That's it. I'm done. If *Ems* did something magical to me before, *baby* knocked me stratospheric. I ease for him. Relax for him. I'll do anything for him, but now all I do is exist as his strong hands glide up my calf and over my knee to massage my thigh. He spends a delicious eternity repeating the unhurried move before switching to my other leg. The process is repeated in its slow entirety. I'm putty in his hands, and as much as I want to touch him, that's apparently not what our moment now is about.

"Turn over," he whispers, and I do.

Gray toys with my hair, brushing it off my shoulders. His fingers trace my spine, running and rubbing my skin, making me squirm. Then he loosens the knot at my neck and the clasp at my back, letting my bikini top fall off even though I'm on my stomach.

"You're perfect. You know that, right?" He draws closer to me.

His body lies parallel but shifts and folds over me. His kiss stuns me when it touches the nape of my neck and slides down my back, following the same path his fingers took. As my skin erupts into shivers, I twist to him, needing so much more, but he holds me in place, kissing my back, all the way to the base of my spine, right to the top of the bikini bottoms.

I lick my lips. "I'm perfect when I'm with you."

He turns me over, my chest bare to him. I don't move to cover or shy away. I've never felt more beautiful than right now. His eyes drink me in, and whatever his fear of the future is, I believe it can be dealt with.

"Sleep with me tonight." His fingertips skim over my skin. "Like *sleep*."

The genuine carefulness in his words stills my heart. I nod. The sun hasn't set, we haven't had dinner, but if he wants to go to bed now, kissing and sleeping until tomorrow, I've never been more ready for bed.

And that's what we do. We kiss and touch and whisper, and long after the sunlight turns to dark, we sleep. His breathing evens out before I tumble into dreams. "I love you, Grayson Ford."

Even though I'm certain he's asleep, his arms flex around me, and this is what happiness means to me.

CHAPTER TEN

EMMA

Saturday night's here, and I'm sitting on Grayson's leg watching Courtney and Ryan lose at beer pong. Maybe it's unnoticeable to anyone else, but Ryan is losing on purpose. He and Courtney have had this thing all week, and it's shifted the looks from Gray and me to them. Thankfully, though, sitting on Gray's leg, letting him run his fingers up and down my arm, I don't care if anyone has an opinion.

The only thing Ryan's said is that it sucks to have a roommate who locks him out of the room, which made me blush. And made Courtney blush. So thinking back on it, Ryan wasn't too pissed at all about Gray commandeering their shared bedroom for nights *with me*. He wanted it for himself.

But right now, heaviness hangs on Grayson's face. It's not obvious, and when pressed for more, all he gives is a placating smile. I can read him well after the days spent together behind closed doors. The sounds I've made for him would be mortifying if not for how amazing they feel. The way his hands play... Grayson's the on-ly person in the world that I'll let see this side of me. The more intimately he touches me, the bolder I am, and when it's my turn, I become more... alive. More me.

Heat hits my cheeks. I know I'm blushing and trying unsuccessfully to hide my smile. Tucking my face into his bare shoulder, I let my lips press to his skin. It warms my memories. I have thoughts of last night with his mouth over me, in between my thighs, and then my first time tasting him... My belly somersaults.

I love it. Love him. Love everything about us.

"What are you smiling at?" His voice tickles my ear.

"Nothing." I might be able to love what we've done, but telling him about my mini-fantasy of wrapping my lips around him and sucking again... Well, I'm going to need a few weeks before I'm comfortable saying that.

He chuckles, and I know he knows. "How about nothing I haven't replayed a hundred times today, too?"

Holy shit, cue belly flip. "Oh my God, Gray."

His hands tighten around my waist, and I squirm. It's becoming one of the things I do most because, when he touches me, I know what comes next.

"Let's get out of here." He lifts me up, and I squeak in giddy surprise. "We're headed to the beach."

Gray heads for the door, holding me against his soapy-scented chest, and grabs a beach blanket from a pile by the door. I'm weightless, supported in his muscular arms. When we hit the sand, I snuggle close. "What are we going to do?"

"What do you want to do, baby?"

"You." I kiss his shoulder.

He clutches me closer, and the scruff from his cheek scratches against my skin. "Just you and me and the ocean right now."

My chest feels tight. The waves crash in the background. The last few days, I've been honest with everything I've said to him. But there have been some thoughts and concerns that have gone unvoiced, mostly about his crazy future fears. "It's romantic."

Distant lights from the beach house give soft shade to his face. "Didn't bring you out here for romance. Just had to get away, be with you."

Gray sets me down and spreads the blanket. In a whoosh, I'm back in his arms, on my back, and he's holding himself over me. But then he rolls us over so I'm on his chest. Forever ticks by, his thick arms clinging to me like he's scared that tomorrow, when we drive home, everything will be forgotten.

He clears his throat. "I have to tell you something."

This again. He starts; then he stops. Whatever *it* is, it's driving him crazy. Me, not so much. Nothing he can say will change how I feel. Young love, maybe. But it's deep. It's burned into my soul.

I prop up on his chest and stare into a face shadowed by the night. "Okay."

"Fuck me." He groans. "I'm not as strong as you think I am."

I nod. "Probably stronger."

"Not like that, Ems. Like… I'm broken inside, and you, you're perfect."

"You're my perfection." He looks away, and I bring his face back to mine. "Just tell me already. Whatever it is, it's killing you and ruining my romance on the beach." Giving him a half-grin and a quiet laugh, I'm dying to help him free himself of this imaginary burden.

"What if we only had tonight?"

I laugh into the salty air. "Well, you know what I'd want." Dropping my mouth to his, I kiss him and let his tongue sweep into my mouth. "The world's ending, and I want you. It's the apocalypse? My last thought is to be next to you, making love to you."

I can't believe I just said that. My blood rushes.

He hugs me close, murmuring against my lips. "You have no idea."

No, I don't. Not if he won't tell me. Instead of pleading with him again, I press my lips to his.

He pulls back. "Emma, I messed up, but I have to wonder if everything happens for a reason. You're going to college. You've got the world lined up—"

That's what his future issue is? "Grayson. Stop."

"It's—"

"Listen." Plastered on his chest, I lean up and cup his cheeks. Breathing in deeply and knowing the truth, I close my eyes and pray whatever hurts him can just heal, that whatever secret he thinks will cause irreparable harm disappears.

"Listening, baby." Even in the dark, his eyes are the most beautiful shade of green I've ever seen.

"I love you, Grayson." My heart seizes. Even though it's the truth, it's out there, and I can't hide or take it back. "You're my best friend, and I'm in love with you."

His eyes search mine in the dark. Silence hangs. Then his hands cup my cheeks, too. We hold each other like that.

"Promise?"

I nod.

"God, baby." He blows out, and I'm not sure whether it's relief or terror. "I love you, too."

Oh, yes. His words are quiet and sweet, but my heart and soul soar. Already lying on top of him, I hug him and bring my gaze back to his. His lips touch mine, and he kisses me. Strong hands rub my back, my bottom. He threads his fingers into my hair. His length hardens between us, and I'm wound so tight, my skin sizzles from the inside out.

"I want this, Gray. I'm giving everything I have to you. Please."

His lips don't leave mine. His hands hold me tighter. "Emma..."

I kiss him. "As long as you never say goodbye to me, we will always be okay in the end. I want you to be my first..." ...and my last, though *that* I don't have the guts to say.

His soft eyelashes sink shut, our bodies meld, and he kisses me back. "I love you."

"Never tell me goodbye."

He stiffens, staring deep into me. Then he blinks, nods, and kisses, his tongue teasing mine. "Ems—"

"Never mind. No more talking. Please?"

With a look so long and deep that it steals my breath, he finally nods and turns me onto my back. It takes seconds for him to remove my bikini, and smiling, I shed him of his shorts. His mouth is on my neck, behind my ear. Warm air blows over us as our hands intertwine. He's so careful with me, kissing me deeply, hugging me close.

"I love you, baby. I do." One hand slips free of our grasp and teases between my legs. He sucks a long breath against my skin, and so do I. Gray teases me until I'm almost grinding against him, and then he presses fingers inside me. It's heaven. It's still so new, so insane, but I've never been more ready for more.

I'm moaning as he works me. "I'm so... Please. Please..."

His mouth meets mine. His hand guides himself close. The head of him touches me, and my heart's pounding. I'm drunk for wanting this, needing him. And as he pushes against me, our eyes lock. "Yes."

"Okay?" he breathes against me.

God, he's holding back, and I'm surging forward. "Please." It's the only thing I can manage. I'm begging. Pleading. The fullness is shocking, the stretching painful. Uncertainty paints his face, but I'm nodding and urging.

"Oh. God." Inch by inch. He moves into me, and my jaw hinges open, my back arching off the blanket. I gulp and gasp.

"Okay?" he says again. Restraint shows in his jaw.

"Don't stop. God." I hurt as much as I love this. The pain abates, and my hips flex toward his. He reads me. He always does. And slowly he slides deeper, only to withdraw and torture me again.

"Fuck me," he groans. "Love this."

I'm without words, but my teeth find his bottom lip, my body's reacting to his, and what happens is more than I can hope for.

I love him. "I love you."

Then Grayson Ford takes over. Slowly, deeply, he rides into me. My legs wrap around him, and he goes faster. My teeth bite into his shoulder, my mind wound tight as my body. When I begin to spiral toward my climax, he knows it. It's an explosion, and we're lost in each other. He comes with me, and it's the best moment of my life, feeling him inside me, feeling me shatter because he made me.

Our breathing levels while slow kisses steal the night away. His hands cover my back, and carefully, he pulls away from me. I'm in his arms, knowing this is how forever feels. Contentment settles in my chest.

Finally, wordlessly, we dress, and I'm back against him. He carries me to bed. It's the middle of the night, maybe close to morning. My eyelids hang in sated, almost-slumber while he arranges the pillows and tucks me in.

"I'll never forget tonight." He kisses my temple, and the comfortable haven of his arms, my pillow, and blanket call to me. "Love you forever."

Slowly, happily, I slip to sleep.

CHAPTER ELEVEN

PRESENT DAY...

GRAYSON

"Go, go, go! Get your asses moving." Orders bark in my earpiece from a man who can't see the shit-storm around Maddox and me.

Mortar fire screams from every direction. Smoke clouds the night air, and my lungs burn. Sulfur burns in my nostrils, and I'm choking on adrenaline. Fight. Survive. Those are my goals. I push against the crumbling wall, breathing hard, wishing like hell there is a break in the insurgent attack we never saw coming.

"Go!"

Shit, man. If we have some place to go, our asses would be moving as ordered. Fuck me. But we are blind, trapped in a dilapidated hut on the outskirts of a town that didn't want us here to begin with.

A bullet hits the wall above me. Another one strikes closer, lower, just a few feet off. I'm not getting shot and left to die in this sandbox. I look over at Maddox, the only other man standing. The ground shakes as a mortar lands outside. Our unit has been decimated. We've got nothing, no ammo, no backup, no support except the asshole in our ears telling us to go.

"Go where?" Maddox shouts. His voice breaks. He's scared. God, man, I'm scared. We're done. No way we see tomorrow. It just can't happen.

"Air support's in there in two minutes. Make it 'til then, boys. You goddamn make it until that bird shows up."

An explosion rocks the hut's roof. It's caving in around us. Dust bites into my eyes. Chunks of plaster rain down. I grab Maddox, pulling him with me, and we run with no idea where to go. We blast through what's left of the door, and cool air smacks me.

I drop, dragging Maddox. All our brothers-in-war died around us, coughing up blood, screaming out in pain. Maddox is in shock. I'd be in the same state of mind, except I long ago lost mine.

"C'mon." I've got him by his shoulder, pushing him to keep my grueling pace. Don't know where we're going, but we gotta get there. Gotta live. I have a plan, have had it for three years. The only thing I need to do is stay alive, fulfill my army contract, and find my way home—to a place almost scarier than war, where memories and mistakes are just as real as bullets and IEDs.

Blasts explode and light the sky. It's yards away and not firing at us. Air support. Fuck me, thank God. Relief floods my mind. I can do this, totally survive this night. Maddox will, too.

"Ford, you there?"

I nod, panting from exertion. "Affirmative, sir."

"Extraction helo coming in hot. Head east, two hundred yards. Remain for pick up."

"Roger that." I signal Maddox; he signals back. There's a wall ahead. We'll be in the open for fifty yards, but we will get to that wall. We'll have partial concealment on the way to our pickup. That's our cover. That's where we can hunker down and breathe. "Ready?"

Maddox gives a thumbs up. He's back, at least enough to run.

"Let's go."

We run. My pulse races as we close in on the wall, and—thump—I turn around. The world slows.

"Gray!" Maddox reaches for me. Even in the dark night, I see his face twist. He's been hit. Mid-run, he's falling down. Blood coats his face, and just that fast, his expression is gone.

"Maddox!" I dive next to his body. "Don't do this, man. We're almost out. C'mon. C'mon!"

His eyes are wide, his mouth open. But he's gone. Dead. I scream into the night. "No! Damn it!"

"Jesus, fuck," comes in my ear. "Ford. Go."

My eyes pinch. Emma. She's the only thing that will get me out of here. I drop and roll, then zigzag toward the pickup location.

A new voice breaks into my earpiece. "Alpha, bravo, one-one, extraction team here. Arriving in one minute, boys."

My throat stings. "Just me. Last man standing."

There's a pause, and for a second, I wonder if they're assessing the risk of picking me up. One man. They've already lost the team. Why risk the helo, the men, all to save one guy? Doom wrecks my hope.

Garbled noise pops in my headset. White noise and static. The earpiece crackles again.

"Roger that, Ford?"

"No. Repeat."

"We're coming in hot, dropping a line. You grab it and tie on. You've got one shot out of hell. You got that, son?"

They're still coming. "Got it."

"Ten seconds."

I fumble for the extraction spot, see the clearing, and run all out.

"Three, two…"

"Here!" The quiet thumps of the stealth chopper arrive.

A line with a hook drops mere yards away. I run after it, pushing my body to reach the only way out of this hellhole. My muscles scream. My head spins. I can't breathe, but I grab the rope. Most of my equipment is gone. I have nothing to secure myself to it. No harness. No carabiners. Shit. Okay. I thread the line through my nylon belt, clip it to itself, then wrap both fists around it. One tug and my body jars in pain as the belt rips into my back, and my feet leave the ground. I hang on, gritting my teeth as the chopper pulls out but stays low.

The wind is harsh. The faster we move, the harder I grip, trying to absorb some of the impact of the line and the feeling of my belt tearing into my back. The chopper pulls right. Then left. We're evading attack. They're protecting me from sniper fire while I'm hanging like some American bull's eye.

I don't know the plan. I can't hear my earpiece any more. Will they pull me up? Will we land and load me in? Whatever they're doing, there's a firefight behind us, and we need to clear the attack zone.

Deep, brilliant, violent pain rips in my side. My nerves scream. I scream. Pain I wasn't expecting overpowers me. Shocks me. I can't hang on. Can't hold myself up. I'm losing my grip. My belt's the only thing that catches me.

Fire burns in my side. I'm shot with no idea how much I'm bleeding. My body dangles and spins out of control on the line. I'm dizzy and dim. Blood is on my tongue, and my life is on my mind. I've done two things wrong in my life: killed my mother and left the girl I loved.

Brutal regret ricochets through my body. The memories I use to fight my hell won't come. Emma's face is dark, blank. I can't remember her kiss, her taste—God, I'm dying. I can't even hear her voice. I've got nothing, no memory of the only girl who made me run, the only one who could save me.

CHAPTER TWELVE

EMMA

"Two minutes, Ginger."

Shit, shoot, shit. The reflection in the mirror isn't doing me any favors tonight. But there isn't time to fix what can't be changed. My hair is sprayed into place, and my boobs are squeezed to look like they are way bigger than they are.

"Ginger!"

God, I hate Wednesday nights. The only thing that can save tonight is... glitter, which I hate. Grabbing the can, I shake it up, close my eyes, and spray down.

My music thumps from above. No way was that two minutes. I have no time to wait for my shimmer to dry. Cursing, I shuffle in shoes that want to kill me and head up the narrow stairs. The higher I climb, the heavier the smoke stinks. My eyes burn, threatening the barely dry fake eyelashes I just glued in place.

"Ginger Raine!" The announcer's baritone still booms through the crappy sound system, making what has to be one of the stupidest stripper names in history echo around me.

"Ta da. I'm here." I wave to Bruno and take in the place.

Packed, even on a weeknight. But it always is. They come to see me. I'm the stupid marquis name. If there ever was a career high point that was completely humiliating, I had that nailed.

This is what I do well. I sell the idea of sex. Of want. Of having an untouchable fantasy.

Because I am one.

Ginger Raine is my only salvation. My biggest secret. She's the once-a-week moneymaker that lets me live my life somewhat comfortably. I've got a future waiting for me, and it has nothing to do with the G-string I'm about to show.

"Work it." Bruno nods as I step onto stage.

The lights are hot. The floor is mine. A hundred eyes are on me, and my smile molds onto my face. It's not even that I'm gorgeous; it's that my smile says so much to the men watching the stage. I learned early on a blink of an eye or a sway of my hips does wicked good things for my wallet.

If it weren't for that, I'd be home and wouldn't hate Wednesdays.

A crescendo of pop beats and bass hits crawl from the speakers. This is work. That's all it is as I mentally drift to another place where I'm dancing for one person, the only boy I ever loved, the only one who ever had me.

What if we just have tonight? The tremble of a memory runs down my spine. Years ago, his hands curled over my naked shoulders, sliding down my bare back, and tonight I drop my head and roll my body remembering how I cried for more. Slowly, my hips sway, remembering the only thing that makes me good at my job.

My eyes close. It's just Grayson and me, all night long. This is my torture every Wednesday. It is also my moneymaker. Bruno says he's never seen a girl bring so much tension to the stage. Guess that's a compliment.

I'm numb to this room. When I drop to my knees, my body lies. It begs each man to touch me, to run their paycheck over my curves. I do it all without seeing a soul.

I'm crawling, gyrating, moaning, and the cash falls. Dollars rain down, and lost in a dream of a man I can never have again, I roll in my take. Fingers scratch my skin as they shove ones into my G-string. My knees slide under the carpet of money as I arch my back. Their bills stick to my skin. Only when the music ends does my autopi-lot trance shut down enough to sway my near-naked ass away.

The night has only just begun. It'd make me sick if I hadn't developed have-no-choice thick skin.

"Give Ginger Raine a few minutes, and she'll be on the floor. If you have a dream, she'll make it come true." The announcer promises the same thing every week to the crowd at the Emerald Gentleman's Club.

I'm their biggest cock tease. No matter what Bruno tries to bait me with and what the an-nouncer promises, I dance, and that's it. Any re-lease that men want can be found on their own.

Bruno is stage left, holding a clove cigarette in his thick fingers. He nods to the beat of the music. "Good girl."

He rocks a Rastafarian look, but it's coupled somehow with a body builder's physique. His bouncers are all similar versions of him. How there's a contingent of Rasta bodybuilders avail-able in the semi-metropolitan area outside Sum-merland, Virginia, I have no idea. But he's found them.

"I try." But I can't keep trying if I don't head downstairs and change.

"Emma." He's blocking my path to the stairs. Tonight, his thick dreads are tied into some ginormous manly bunch at the back of his head, making him seem every bit the dread-head owner. He's sexy. He knows it. His powerful body is in a tailored suit that hangs perfectly on his bulky muscles. Between that and owning this place, his ego is as big as his personality.

Almost every girl to walk onto his stage has been with him, not because he makes it a requirement but because they can't stay away. Until they never come back. It's not a job for the stable, even if Emerald's Gentlemen Club is about as high class as exists around here. It's not a profession that screams lengthy job history. My two years with Bruno are outliers, and because of that, we've developed a rapport. In his own way, he cares.

"Where's your head tonight? You went deeper than normal."

My sad smile tells him everything he needs to know. Bruno never flirts with me. My guess would be because he knows most of my story. For as hard as he acts, I think he actually wants to help. Why else would he have hired me back in the day when my body was a little soft?

"Just doing the gig."

"You're too young." He shakes his head. "To live like you're that old."

It's almost like he wants to fix my past by supporting my future. I don't know if that even makes sense. It's just what it is. I'm his marquis girl, so he wants to take care of his meal ticket.

But he's also convinced that being twenty means that eventually, I need to let loose and party *with* someone, preferably one of the patrons. That way he'd make a little, I'd get a little, and everyone would be happy. In his mind, a good old-fashioned, screaming orgasm—from a *person,* not a vibrator—would be life altering.

Well, no thank you. Did that once, and it *was* life altering. That's about as much paradigm shift as I could handle.

"I need a couple minutes, Bruno. Seriously, I'm fine, and I promise I'll make us good money."

His hand lands on my shoulder, and his fingers give me a squeeze. "You raked in more money in the last hour than ever before."

"Yay, me. That's a good thing. Right?"

He smirks sarcastically. "Emma, you cleaned out wallets. So I know you're in your head."

"You give me this same speech every week."

Nodding, he looks over my shoulder. "Just want to keep you working for as long as possible."

"Got it."

"And..." He paints on a smile that can only mean vulgarity ahead. "If you feel the need to blow someone, make him pay first."

"I'll remember that." My eyes roll. The shit that comes out of his mouth is so foul that it's not. Sex is business. To Bruno, it's no different buying someone an ice cream, a Rolex, or an orgasm. Each provides pleasure.

He moves aside, and I teeter-totter down the stairs, heading to my vanity. A quick once-over of my makeup and that damn glitter spray, and I'm good. I check my phone. It's blinking with a text message from Cherry. She knows I'm at work, and my stomach drops.

Cherry: *Call me.*

Shit. I swipe the screen and call back. My mind's running fast as the music's dropping upstairs. The phone's ringing, and I'm trying to stay grounded. *Nothing's wrong.* I tie on my corset and slip on some thigh-highs. No answer, voice mail.

Biting my lip, I think, it's probably nothing, but my heart's beating faster. "Hey, it's me. Just checking on everything. Call me back."

The room feels like it's closing in, but if something was really wrong, Cherry would've called and texted something like SOS or ASAP. Something. Anything. I grab a black see-through robe and sash it so my boobs are on display.

My phone rings, and I jump for it. "Cherry? Everything okay—"

"Emma, oh my God."

My pulse skyrockets. "What?"

"We went for ice cream. I saw Julie, who was with Trevor and—"

"Cherry, *what*?"

"Grayson Ford's unit was attacked. They said no one survived." Cherry's voice cracks. "I'm so sorry."

I falter, stumbling back to my chair. "God..."

Bile churns in my stomach. I want to be sick. I want to run away from tonight, throw my phone away, and pretend what she said is wrong, that he's just far away, never to be heard from. Death is final. My hopes... I always had hopes. "Oh, God..."

Footsteps creak at the top of the stairs. "Emma. Get up here. Folks are restless."

I swallow over the lump in my throat. "Okay... I have to go."

Ending the call, I'm numb. But I have to go to work. I need to... just do something. Otherwise, the overwhelming loss might kill me in my chair. "Coming."

Slowly, I push back up the stairs and zero in on my prospects for the night. It's easy to map who'll be up for private time. I can close my eyes and hide my tears. I've lost my Grayson, but at least I have our daughter.

** Coming Soon: *Only For Her*, the next installment in the Only series. To ensure you do not miss Grayson and Emma's story, please text **TITAN** to **66866** to sign up for exclusive emails or visit **www.CristinHarber.com**. **

ABOUT THE AUTHOR

Cristin Harber is a *New York Times* and *USA Today* bestselling romance author. She writes sexy, steamy romantic suspense, military romance, new adult, and contemporary romance. Readers voted her onto Amazon's Top Picks for Debut Romance Authors in 2013, and her debut Titan series was both a #1 romantic suspense and #1 military romance bestseller.

Join the newsletter! Text TITAN to 66866 to sign up for exclusive emails or visit www.CristinHarber.com

The Only Series:
Book 1: Only for Him
Book 2: Only for Her
Book 3: Only for Us
Book 4: Only Forever

The Delta Series:
Book 1: Delta: Retribution
Book 2: Delta: Revenge (releases in 2015)

The Titan Series:

Book 1: Winters Heat

Book 1.5: Sweet Girl

Book 2: Garrison's Creed

Book 3: Westin's Chase

Book 4: Gambled

Book 5: Chased

Book 6: Savage Secrets

Book 7: Hart Attack

Book 8: Black Dawn (releases in 2015)

Each Titan and Delta book can be read as a standalone (except for Sweet Girl), but readers will likely best enjoy the series in order.

ACKNOWLEDGEMENTS

Thank you, readers! The Only series is a new adventure for me. The overwhelming support I've received has been amazing. I felt this story deep in my soul and couldn't let go of the characters. They've pushed me to write differently, to explore new ways of storytelling, and for that I'm forever grateful.

Thank you and huge tackle hugs to Team Titan. Each day you make me laugh and smile. I love your support and willingness to try something new. You will never know how much your messages, posts, tweets, shares, and reviews means to me.

Each day I get to work with amazing authors whose opinions I cannot live without. Thank you for your advice, your time, and your considerable strength: JB Salsbury, Racquel Reck, Claudia Connor, and Sharon Kay. I am forever a friend and in awe of each of you.

Another huge thank you to the team that makes my dreams come true. Thank you to Julia Sutherland for your heart and your time, to Red Adept and Jacy's Red Ink for editing and proofing, to Okay Creations and Sarah Hansen for creating a cover that is brilliantly beautiful, and to Inkslinger PR— KP Simmon, Tara Gonzalez, and Amber Noffke— for the creative energy that you ignite.

Finally, thank you to my family who supports me without   hesitation.

42632603R00076

Made in the USA
Middletown, DE
17 April 2017